序言

　　「學習兒童美語系列教材」，係**引進國外最新資訊**，結合多位優秀資深的中外編輯及兒童美語教師，完全針對兒童心理，誘發學習潛能，傾力編輯而成。

　　中國小孩應該擁有一套屬於自己的美語教材，在最自然而值得驕傲的本土環境中，開口說ABC。學習出版公司即堅守**國情化、本土化、趣味化**的編纂原則，排除萬難，投下巨大人力財力，以期貢獻兒童美語教學界一份真正好用好學的教材，為中國的孩子們盡一些棉薄之力。

　　為了方便教師及家長對這套屬於國人自己的美語教材，有更進一步的使用認識，特編著此一教師手冊，將學習兒童美語讀本的教學方式與學生可能遭遇的學習困難，一一條列，便於參考查閱，並附有習題解答，使教師與家長能掌握教學方向，並進而控制教學效果、啓發兒童的學習潛力。

編者　謹識

學習兒童美語系列

- 學習語言的基本順序，是由 Hearing（聽）、Speaking（說）、Reading（讀）、Writing（寫），本套教材即依此原則編輯。

- 將英語歌曲、遊戲，具有創意的美勞，與學習英語巧妙地組合在一起，以提高兒童的學習興趣，達到**寓敎於樂**的目的。

- 全套系列包括 Workbook ①-⑥、KK音標及自然發音法①②，可供老師搭配使用，效果更佳。

- 本套書以六歲兒童到國二學生為對象，是全國唯一與國中英語課程相銜接的美語教材。學完六冊的小朋友，上了國中，既輕鬆又愉快。

CONTENTS

Book 1 —•

Book 2 —•

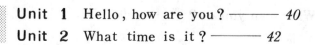

Book 3 ——•

Book 4

Book 5

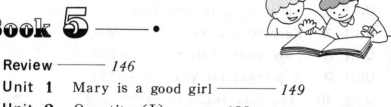

Book 6

LEARNING
English Readers for Children 1

Unit 1

Greetings

♠ 學習目標

能將Good morning, Good afternoon, Good evening 等問候語，流利地應用於日常生活中。

♠ 教學方式

(1)將morning, afternoon, evening, night 等字獨立練習至純熟，並讓學生瞭解所代表之不同時段。

(2)解釋 "Good" 為 "好" 的意思，而 "Good morning" 為問候別人早上好，意即「早安」。其餘類推。

♠ 教學重點

(1) "Good evening" 與 "Good night" 在中文均為晚安，學生容易混淆，前者為晚上見面時之問候，而 "Good night" 為「夜安」，為睡前之道別。

(2)在學生未能將上述問候語練習純熟以前，勿讓學生加上彼此之英文名字對練，以免增加其記憶發音之困難，與開口練習之恐懼。

♠ 活　動

(1)反覆如 "Good morning, students." "Good morning, teacher." 等對話練習，老師前導，讓學生跟讀，以收示範與糾正發音之效，並實際應用於每次上課，時與學生相互問候。

⑵可將學生分為二組，按前後座位順序每組一人至黑板作指字
　或指圖比賽，以提高其學習興趣。

⑶可準備一活動時鐘（以後教 Time 時亦可使用），老師（或
　稍後可指定學生）撥動時針至不同時段，讓全體學生辨認
　回答，亦可以⑵法玩競答遊戲。

習題解答

1-1 LET'S PRACTICE（p.2）

Good morning, students.
Good morning, Ma'am.

Good afternoon, Mary.
Good afternoon, John.

Good evening, John.
Good evening, Susan.

Good night, John.
Good night, Mary.

Unit 2

What's your name?

♠ 學習目標

能詢問他人及回答自己的名字。

♠ 教學方式

(1) 對年紀稍大，理解程度較強之學生，可先解釋 " What's " 即是 " What is " ， " What's your name ? " 的字面解釋為 " 什麼是你的名字 " ，按中文之語法即為「你叫什麼名字」。而對年紀較小之學生，則以韻律背誦，引導其能朗朗上口為先。

(2) 先將所有格 my ， your ， his ， her 等字反覆練習至能清楚辨認，再加入句型練習，以減低記憶太多生字的困難。

♠ 教學重點

年紀稍小之學生，易混淆 what , is , name 與所有格等生字，故一次不宜介紹太多。可先練習 " What's your name ? My name is _____ . What's your name ? " 並強調二個 your 語調的不同，如 " What's your name ? " 與 What's your name ?

♠ 練 習

(1) 教師可用此課來讓學生熟悉自己與同學之名字。先用中文點名，讓學生練習說 " Here " ，再詢問之 " What's your name ? " 學生則回答 " My name is _____ . "

(2) 上述練習熟練流利之後教師先示範"My name is_____."
指定一學生起立並詢問"What's your name?",該生回
答,並由其指定另一位同學作同樣的練習,直到每一人均
演練過爲止。

(3) 利用遊戲——打擊魔鬼來練習。先熟悉自己與同學的名字,
並選派一自願者當鬼。老師可先問"What's your name?"
該生回答之後,再問全體同學"What's his/her name?"
全體回答"His/Her name is_____." 準備一有聲之
塑膠槌或紙筒,喊出另一學生之名字,讓魔鬼持紙筒敲擊。
被喊到之學生可在魔鬼敲擊前,速喊他人之名字,魔鬼則
轉而追擊他人。凡未能及時轉喊他人名字之學生,必須接
替成爲新魔鬼。每一次新魔鬼產生時,教師可做遊戲開始
前的問答練習。
如此數次之後,學生可牢記自己之名字,並認識其他同學。

習題解答

2-1 LET'S PRACTICE
(p.5)

What's his name?
His name is Mark.

What's her name?
Her name is Susan.

What's her name?
Her name is Nancy.

What's his name?
His name is Jack.

Unit 3,4

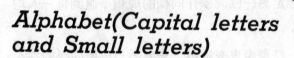

Alphabet(Capital letters and Small letters)

♠ 學習目標

能辨認各大小寫字母，年紀較大之學生可開始書寫之練習。

♠ 教學方式

(1)在黑板上依大小寫將字母按序寫好，依序領讀數遍之後，可跳讀（不按順序）練習至熟讀，再指定學生 one by one 到黑板作指認練習，或分二組競答。

(2)待學生作完上述練習對字母已略具印象後，將課本上之圖卡製作成稍大之字母卡，讓學生辨認，教師手指圖卡反覆領讀。字母部份，可以抽卡回答的方式作遊戲。

♠ 教學重點

(1)圖卡之生字部份，對初學者而言，內容多不易學，可分成數組教完，以免學生記憶困難。

(2)單元㈢中之大寫 I，印刷體為 I 易與 L 之小寫 l 混淆，應促請學生寫成 I 。

(3)單元㈣之小寫 b，d 與 p，q 等字母，學生易寫錯，應加強此 4 個字母之辨認。

♠ 練 習

(1)可以遊戲方式將圖卡分給學生，每人一張（圖朝下），被點到之學生起立，將圖卡翻開，並唸出來，唸對者可得一分。可分兩組記分競賽。

(2)可將某些生字如BANANA（or banana）寫在黑板上,問學生有幾個A／a 有幾個B／b 等等。

(3)如學習目標,將圖卡分給學生,任選一圖卡中之生字寫於黑板,讓學生將圖卡翻過來,例如DOG／dog 則拿到字母D,O與G／d,o 與 g 之學生須出列,並按序站立,將圖卡拿好,如此可在趣味中增加對字母與生字之記憶。

3-3 EXERCISE (p.11)

4-1 LET'S PRACTICE (p. 14)

Fill in the small letters.

4-3 EXERCISE (p.16)

1. Draw a circle.

An apple ?	A cat ?	A fish ?
(Yes) No	Yes (No)	(Yes) No
A king ?	A tiger ?	An egg ?
Yes (No)	Yes (No)	(Yes) No

2. Fill the blanks.

1. b c d
2. e f g
3. h i j
4. r s t
5. w x y

3. Look and join.

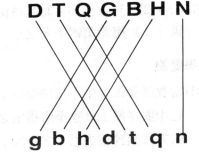

D T Q G B H N

g b h d t q n

Unit 5

Numbers(1～10)

♠ 學習目標

學習數字1至10之唸法與寫法。

♠ 教學方式

(1)以口頭方式,讓學生大聲跟讀1到10至朗朗上口。隨著練習次數之增加可加快其速度,學生很快的便能將1至10依序背誦出來。

(2)將1,2,…10等數字依序寫於黑板上,此時將速度放慢,並糾正學生之發音。再將數字不依序排列於黑板上以教學桿指讀直到學生可以不依序辨認讀出。

(3)(1)、(2)法熟讀後方可將其拼法抄寫出來,並要求學生拼讀各數字,以複習第㈣單元之小寫字母。

♠ 教學重點

(1)當教師要求學生不依序唸時,會發現大部份學生,仍會先在心中依序從1默唸至所指定之數字再大聲說出來。可以競答的方式訓練縮短思考之時間,而能將數字獨立記憶。

(2) Three 中〔θ〕之音學生易發爲〔s〕之音,須注意上下牙齒須輕咬住舌尖以發此音。另 seven 之〔v〕,學生多錯發爲〔m〕之音,〔sɪks〕讀成〔sɛks〕,five 漏掉了尾音〔v〕而唸成〔faɪ〕,亦應多加注意並糾正。

♠ 練 習

(1)讓學生靜坐並閉上眼睛，第一個被老師拍到肩膀之學生大聲喊出 one，第二個則喊 Two ，如此依序練習。因學生不知何時輪到自己被拍，故較能集中注意力並加深記憶。

(2)可依課本 17 頁，將學生分組，每次二人至黑板競寫出老師所唸之數字（僅寫出阿拉伯數字）。或每人準備一張紙，隨意寫下自己喜愛的數字，由老師任喊一數字，與所喊數字相同者須馬上起立，淘汰錯誤與起立較慢者。剩下者每人再重寫一數字，如此反覆數次練習。

(3)將阿拉伯數字與英文拼寫不依序分寫於黑板兩側，分二組輪流指派一學生（或自願），將教師所唸之數字以連連看的方式作遊戲，連對者該組可得一分。

習題解答

5-3
EXERCISE
（ p. 21 ）

1 two oranges	2 eight apples
3 five hats	4 nine pencils
5 three dogs	6 ten eggs
7 seven trees	8 three girls
9 four Indian boys	10 six cats

Unit 6

Numbers (11~100)

♠ 學習目標

學習數字的讀與寫，並廣泛應用於生活中數字有關的事物上。

♠ 教學方式

(1) 複習數字 1 至 10，加上 11 與 12，作 1 至 12 的數字練習。

(2) 如下法：

3. three	13. thirteen	30. thirty
4. four	14. fourteen	40. fourty
⋮	⋮	⋮
9. nine	19. nineteen	90. ninety

將數字寫於黑板上，並將 teen 與 ty 用紅筆標示出來，並告訴學生除了 11 與 12 外，十幾的說與寫法均是加上 teen，幾十則加上 ty。

(3) 另列一表：

2. two	12. twelve	20. twenty
3. three	13. thirteen	30. thirty
5. five	15. fifteen	50. fifty

指出 2 為例外，以及 3 , 5 加上 teen 或 ty 時的發音與寫
法之不同。

♠ 活　動

(1)老師可將自己之電話號碼寫在黑板上，示範其唸法（先唸
前三碼，暫停，再唸後四碼）。指定學生回家練習說自己
的電話號碼，並於下次上課抽問。

(2)指定 2 個男生，請他們幫老師用英文從不同方向數班上共
有幾個男生。然後老師帶領全體同學一齊數，確認是否正
確。稍後可指定女生作同樣的練習。

♣ 教學重點

(1) teen 與 ty 之發音相近，以致學生可能將 13 與 30 等唸成
一樣。應注意 teen 為重音所在，長且帶〔n〕之鼻音，而
ty 短而弱，可以對比方式多作練習。

(2) hundred 為百，必要時 thousand（千），zero（零）的說法
亦可一併提示，以滿足學生的好奇心。

習題解答

6-3 EXERCISE (p. 26)

A. (1) *three six nine — seven two eight four*

(2) *nine four two — five three three six*

(3) *three four one — five six eight nine*

B. (1) *It is eleven dollars.*

(2) *It is fourteen dollars.*

(3) *It is twenty-three dollars.*

6-2 PLAY A GAME

Join, point and say. (p. 25)

Unit 7

What time is it?

♠ 教學方式

(1) 將What 獨立解釋，並說明疑問副詞必須放於句子的開頭，故不能將中文的「現在幾點」，說成" It is what time？" 而應是" What time is it？" 領讀並練習至每一學生均能開口發問。

(2) 先用阿拉伯數字，練習直說法，如1：30為" It's one-thirty." 使學生能先以簡單方式回答時間。

♠ 活 動

(1) 準備一活動指鐘，反覆作時間辨認的練習。

(2) 可指派一生，撥動指針，並由其詢問另一生" What time is it？"該生回答後，由其撥定時間再指定另一生作同樣之問答練習。

♠ 教學重點

(1) 學生若對數字之英文拼寫與辨認有學習困難，可先以阿拉伯數字作練習，稍後再視學習狀況加入。

7-1 LET'S PRACTICE (p.29)

Look at the clock and write the time.

① It's five o'clock.

② It's nine o'clock.

③ It's four o'clock.

④ It's three o'clock.

⑤ It's twelve forty.

⑥ It's one twenty.

7-3 EXERCISE (p.31)

A. 1. *It's eleven o'clock.*

2. *It's ten fifteen, or It's fifteen after ten.*

3. *It's twelve thirty.*

B.

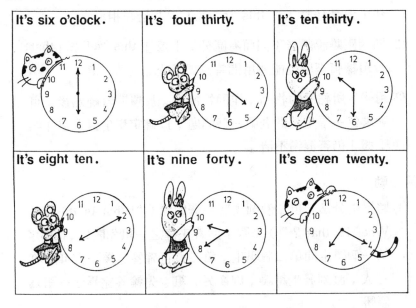

It's six o'clock.	It's four thirty.	It's ten thirty.
It's eight ten.	It's nine forty.	It's seven twenty.

Unit 8

What is this?
What is that?

♠ 教學方式

(1) 如同上一單元所提過的，疑問副詞須放在句首，與中文語法「這是什麼」" This is what ? "恰好相反。

(2) 將因距離說話者不同而有區分的「這」this 與「那」that，反覆練習至學生能運用問答無誤爲止。

(3) 用學生所熟悉的物品，作問答練習。反覆問答純熟後，可要求每一學生反問老師一個問題，以確定學生對「這」與「那」仍否混淆不清。

♠ 活　動

(1) 將學生分爲二組，教師先問一個問題（ "What is this ? / What is that ? ")先舉手回答正確之一組先開始，按座序第一個學生問第二個學生，第二人正確答完後，方可問第三人，直到發生錯誤，則換另一組。先輪答完畢之一組爲優勝。

(2) 亦可運用教字母之圖卡分給學生，讓其一一上台，說明自己拿到之圖卡爲何物。

♠ 教學重點

(1)〔ð〕之音學生易發爲〔l〕之音，應注意糾正。

(2) an 的用法可告訴學生們,如果單字的第一個字母為母音時,
便要用 an 而不用 a ,以及母音有 a,e,i,o,u 等 5 個,使
學生有概念即可,不必解釋太詳細,以免學生發生困惑。

習題解答

8-1 LET'S PRACTICE (p.34)
What is this ?

Fill in the blanks.

8-3 EXERCISE (p.36)

A. Questions and answers.

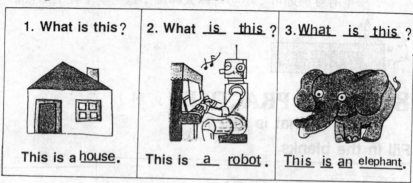

1. What is this?	2. What _is_ _this_?	3. What _is_ _this_?
This is a <u>house</u>.	This is <u>a</u> <u>robot</u>.	<u>This is an</u> <u>elephant</u>.

B. Draw and write.

1. Draw a pencil.	2. Draw a fish.	3. Draw ice cream.
This is <u>a pencil</u>.	This <u>is a fish</u>.	<u>This is ice cream</u>.

Unit 9

Is this a ball?

♠ 教學方式

(1) 首先複習單元㈧之 " This is a _____ ." 與 " That is a _____ ." 練習至學生們能陳述無誤，並能區分因距離不同，而使用 this 或 that。

(2) 將敘述句與疑問句上、下並列如 { " This is a book." " Is this a book？" }
並將 this, is 等字用紅筆標示出來，讓學生明瞭，將直述句中的 be 動詞移到句首，便可形成疑問句。

(3) 將直述句 " This is a book." 與否定句 " This is not a book." 並列，並於 is 與 is not 下加註紅線，要求學生練習「是」為 is, 不是則如同中文須加個「不」not, is not 為「不是」。

♠ 活 動

(1) 將 not, is, This, a 等字與數個學生已學習過之生字，抄在黑板上，可不依序地編上號碼，教師選擇直述、疑問或否定句型之一，讓學生們以重組方式來玩遊戲。可要求學生齊答，亦可分二組競答。

(2) 在黑板上抄上三至四個生字，然後選一個學生出列，背對黑板，教師將所指定的字，用粉筆圈起來，背對黑板的學生便可以 " Is this a _____？" 的方式來詢問團體同學。如果猜錯了或問錯了，則同學們回答 No, it is not a _____。如果二次詢問均猜不中便出局。二次內猜中的，同學們則須回答 " Yes, it is a _____. " 該生所代表之一組便得一分。此練習的趣味性，可使學生更熟悉本單元之句型。

♠ 教學重點

部分學生將 " This is not a boy. " 翻譯成「這是不是一個男生」，故須注意勿將 not 解釋成不是，而強調 is 爲「是」，is not 爲「不是」，以免學生混淆。

9-1 LET'S PRACTICE (p.39)

Is this a bicycle ?

No, it is not.
It is not a bicycle.
It is a car.

Is this an eraser ?

Yes, it is.
It is an eraser.

Is this a table ?

No, it is not.
It is not a table.
It is a blackboard.

Is this a duck ?

No, it is not.
It is not a duck.
It is a chicken.

Is this a fish ?

No, it is not.
It is not a fish.
It is a bird.

Is this a cake ?

Yes, it is.

It is a cake.

Is this a tiger ?

No, it is not.
It is not a tiger.
It is a cat.

Is this a piano ?

Yes, it is.

It is a piano.

9-3 EXERCISE (p. 41)

1. Is this a book ? Yes, it is. It is _a_ _book_ .	**2. Is this a flower ?** No, it is not. It is not _a_ _flower_ . It _is_ _an_ umbrella .
3. Is this a pencil ?  _Yes_ , it is. It is _a_ _pencil_ .	**4. Is this _a_ table ?** No, _it_ _is_ _not_ . It is _not_ _a_ _table_ . It _is_ _a_ _desk_ .
5. _Is_ _this_ _a_ chair ?  _Yes_ , _it_ _is_ . _It_ _is_ _a_ chair .	**6. Is** _this_ _a_ telephone ? _No_ , _it_ _is_ _not_ . It _is_ not a _telephone_ . It _is_ _a_ _bag_ .

Unit 10,11

Parts of my body (I)(II)

♠ 教學方式

(1) 單元㈩與㈪所包括身體各部份的名稱很多，應先衡量總上課時數，再平均分配，最好能依上、下及不同部位來教，如可分頭、上半身、下半身、與四肢等，學生較能記憶及學習。

(2) 首先運用自己的身體來練習。老師可以指著自己的鼻子說 nose，學生自然也會跟著指著自己的鼻子重覆唸，如此反覆練習。然後教師可只指某一部位，讓學生們回答。

(3) 對身體各部份名稱熟悉之後，再加入句子練習。對 This is my _____ . 的句型熟悉後，可視學生的學習能力，加入單元㈠的 your，his, her 等作練習。教師可與學生互練，亦可由學生對答。

♠ 活 動

(1) 教師可指定不同之部位，要求學生用手指出來。稍為熟練後，教師可故意指錯部位，來試驗那些只是看著別人的動作而跟著作的學生。然後加上 " Teacher says, touch your nose." 學生方可摸自己的鼻子，若無 " Teacher says "，則不須作動作，如同中式遊戲「老師說」。

(2)可利用單元(八)所教過之疑問句與否定句讓學生作練習，依座序站起來回答，教師可指著第一個學生的手問 " Is this your leg? " 使其回答 " No, this is not my leg. This is my hand. "，答完後必須問第二個學生一個問題，直到每個學生均練習過並能流利運用。

♠ **教學重點**

學生易將 mouth 發為 mouse 之音，老師可強調其中文意思之差別，別把「嘴巴」說成「老鼠」。

習題解答

A. Look at the picture and circle the correct word.

10-3
EXERCISE
（p.46）

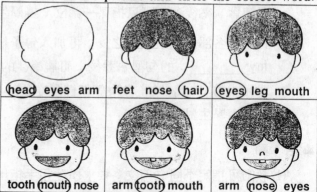

| (head) eyes arm | feet nose (hair) | (eyes) leg mouth |
| tooth (mouth) nose | arm (tooth) mouth | arm (nose) eyes |

B. Draw and write.

此練習由老師要求學生畫上自己的臉，然後寫上各部位的英文名稱。

11-1 LET'S PRACTICE (p. 49)

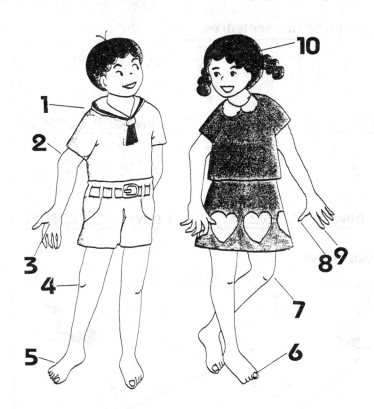

1. shoulder	6. toe
2. arm	7. leg
3. hand	8. thumb
4. knee	9. finger
5. foot	10. hair

11-3 EXERCISE (p. 51)

A. Complete the sentences.

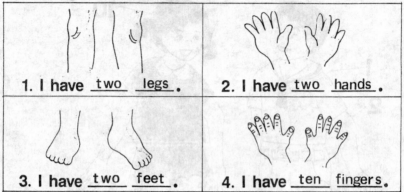

1. I have <u>two</u> <u>legs</u>.
2. I have <u>two</u> <u>hands</u>.
3. I have <u>two</u> <u>feet</u>.
4. I have <u>ten</u> <u>fingers</u>.

B. Join lines.

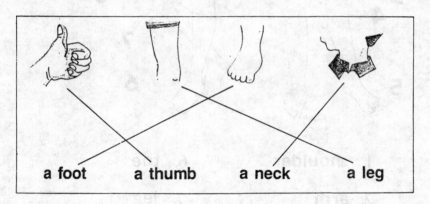

a foot   a thumb   a neck   a leg

Unit 12

My family

♠ 教學方式

(1)將本單元生字 mother, father, sister, 與 brother 領讀並解釋中文意思與其關係。

(2)複習單元㈠之句型 "This is my ＿＿＿＿." , 再加入本課之生字 , 在黑板上寫下 " This is my ＿＿＿＿." 之句型 , 反覆練習。

♠ 活　動

(1)可讓小朋友指著課本上之圖卡練習 , 亦可以 4 或 5 個小朋友一組 , 有些人扮 mother, father, sister, brother 等 , 輪流互相介紹。

(2)可指定小朋友回家準備全家福照片一張 , 於下次上課帶來 , 輪流介紹自己的家人讓同學認識。

♠ 教學重點

M**o**ther 之母音發〔ʌ〕 , 而 F**a**ther 發〔ɑ〕音 , 二者易混淆 , 切不可將 Mother 發爲〔ˈmɑðə〕。

12-1 LET'S PRACTICE (p.54)

This is my sister.

This is my mother.

This is my father.

This is my sister.

My name is John.

12-3 EXERCISE (p.56)

```
┌─────────────────┐
│                 │
│   Paste your    │
│  photo here.    │
│                 │
└─────────────────┘
```

My name is _____ .

```
┌─────────────────┐
│    Paste        │
│  your father's  │
│    photo        │
│    here.        │
└─────────────────┘
```
```
┌─────────────────┐
│    Paste        │
│  your mother's  │
│    photo        │
│    here.        │
└─────────────────┘
```

This is my <u>father</u>.   *This is <u>my</u> <u>mother</u>.*

```
┌─────────────────┐
│    Paste        │
│ your brother's  │
│    photo        │
│    here.        │
└─────────────────┘
```
```
┌─────────────────┐
│    Paste        │
│ your sister's   │
│    photo        │
│    here.        │
└─────────────────┘
```

This <u>is</u> <u>my</u> <u>brother</u>.   *This <u>is</u> <u>my</u> <u>sister</u>.*

Unit 13

I am…. You are….

♠ 教學方式

(1)將 boy（男生）與 girl（女生）練習至能區分無誤，讓男生一起跟讀 "I am a boy." 女生則練習 "I am a girl."

(2)首先使學生一一至台前作自我介紹，練習說自己的名字 "I am _____." 與性別 "I am a boy / girl." 並利用這個機會讓學生熟悉他人的名字。老師可於每個學生介紹完畢後說 "This is _____." 以加強介紹這位同學，並示範其名字之正確發音，直到每個人均能正確地說出自己與他人的名字。

♠ 活 動

(1)選一個小朋友至台前，並在其對立之另一組中，選三～四個小朋友於坐位起立，簡單自我介紹如上述教學方式(2)，再由台前之小朋友說 "This is _____." 若四人均能介紹無誤，則算過關（或得分），再由另一組選派小朋友作同樣練習，或分組計分競賽。

(2)為了讓學生彼此認識，並訓練其上課時集中注意力，可利用此一活動加強其記憶能力。由第一個學生說出自己的名字後，第二人重覆第一人之名字，並加上自己的名字，第三人則重覆一、二人之名字，並加上自己之名字，以此類推。至第二輪時，第一人重覆所有人之名字，並加上一物，第二人除了重覆第一人所述外，亦須加上一物，其餘類推。凡陳述有誤或遺漏者，則退出遊戲。最後剩下者為勝利者。

習題解答

John

I am <u>John</u>.
I am <u>a</u> <u>boy</u>.

Mary

I am <u>Mary</u>.
I <u>am</u> <u>a</u> <u>girl</u>.

You are <u>Mary</u>.
<u>You</u> <u>are</u> <u>a</u> <u>girl</u>.

You <u>are</u> <u>John</u>.
<u>You</u> <u>are</u> <u>a</u> <u>boy</u>.

Draw yourself here.

<u>I</u> <u>am</u> ～. (What is your name?)

<u>I</u> <u>am</u> <u>a</u> ～. (Are you a boy or a girl?)

Unit 14

He is…. She is….

♠ 教學方式

(1) 將 boy，girl，man，woman 等生字與中文意義練習純熟。

(2) 將 " What is she / he？" 之句型抄寫於黑板上，並解釋
詢問別人職業（亦即工作）時以 "What " 來問。

(3) 將 teacher（老師），policeman（警察），doctor（醫生），
nurse（護士），farmer（農夫），mailman（郵差）等六
種職業領讀數遍，待學生大致能記憶後，教師可指著圖卡問
" What is she / he？" 而由學生們回答 " He / She is a
_____．"

♠ 活動

(1) 可準備寫有 teacher，policeman，doctor，nurse，farmer 與
mailman 等字之卡片數張，分給學生一人一張，然後點二位
學生於坐位起立，互相問 " What are you？" 答 " I am
a _____．" 問答皆無誤者方可坐下。

♠ 教學重點

本單元所練習之 " He is _____．" " She is _____．"
可與單元㈠之所有格一併比較練習，如：" She is Mary．=
Her name is Mary．" 如學生年紀稍大，可略為介紹主格與
所有格在文法上之不同，將其整理如下表，以方便學生記憶。

主　格	所　有　格
I （我）	My （我的）
You （你）	your （你的）
He （他）	His （他的）
She （她）	Her （她的）

習題解答

14-1
LET'S
PRACTICE
（p. 64）

John 　　Mary 　　Mr. Lee 　　Mrs. Ling 　　Mark	1. He is _a_ _boy_. He is _John_.
2. She is _a_ _girl_. She is _Mary_.	3. He is Mr. Lee. He is a man .
4. She is Mrs. Ling. She is a woman.	5. He is Mark . He is a boy .

14-3 EXERCISE (p. 66)

1.

He
She is a （boy,）
girl.

2.

He
（She） is a man.
（woman.）

3.

He
（She） is a doctor.
（nurse,）

4.

（He）
She is a mailman.
（farmer,）

5.

He
（She） is a nurse.
（teacher.）

總複習

　　在教完第一冊所安排的幾個單元後，學生們可說是踏出了學習英文穩健的第一步。對英語初學者而言，語言的教學重於語文的訓練，亦即會聽、會說，比會寫來得重要而且實際。故在複習這幾個單元之時，切莫讓拼寫生字之困難，扼殺了學生們學習語言之興趣。這一點對年紀稍小之初學者，尤為重要。

習題解答

R-3 LOOK AND WRITE（p.69）

1. a cat
2. a dog
3. a fish
4. a boy
5. a hat
6. an umbrella
7. the sun
8. a duck
9. a hen
10. a kite
11. two birds
12. a chair
13. a house
14. a bicycle
15. a car
16. a flower
17. a bee
18. a girl

R-4
A CROSSWORD PUZZLE （p.70）

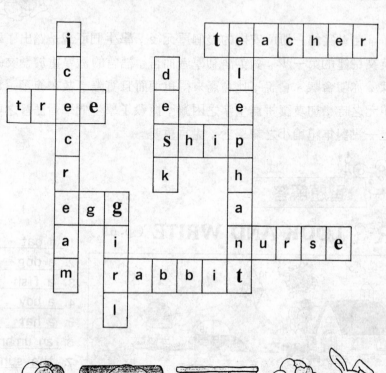

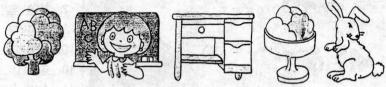

LEARNING
English Readers for Children 2

Let's Start with English

Hello, How Are You ?

♠ 教學方式

(1) 從本單元開始，學生們開始進入學習比較有序的對話練習，可先讓學生仔細聽老師的示範後再跟讀，直到學生能對句子的韻律熟悉而能朗朗上口。

(2) 因本單元的句型在第一冊均出現過，只需稍做解釋加強印象，即可讓學生做模擬之對話練習。

無論在以練習或遊戲方式的進行中，學生如有錯誤，不要立即糾正，以免打斷學生整組練習之連貫性，待一組練習完後，再分別指出錯誤之處，給予指導與糾正。

♠ 練 習

(1) 將對話中之人物 Mark，Susan 與 Mary 分別以 A，B，C 代號代替，以老師示範對話中之人物 A，另選二位小朋友分別為 B 與 C。

第二次練習時，B 的同學則扮 A，C 則扮 B 並由 C 選一位同學扮人物 C，並將課本中之人物名改為自己的英文名字，如此反覆練習至每位小朋友都練習過為止。

(2) 將小朋友三人一組分配好，指定其以話劇方式練習為家庭作業，下次上課前，可給予其 10 分鐘排練，要求每位小朋友均能不看課本而能演練，可以比賽方式，對表現最優之幾組給予獎勵。

♠教學重點

因英語畢竟不是母語，小朋友接觸複習的機會除了課堂外並不多，適時要求對話背誦，可幫助其熟悉與記憶較長與困難之句型。

Unit 2

What Time Is It?

♠ 教學方式

(1) 首先將這個單元的生字 half 與 quarter 分別解釋，half 爲一半，即 ½，而 quarter 爲 ¼ 的意思，運用在時間上即是有半小時與 15 分鐘（即一小時的 ½ 與 ¼），必要時可利用圖形輔助。

(2) 在黑板上畫二個時鐘，解釋以 6 與 12 所畫之直線爲界，右半邊，即半小時以前，用幾點過幾分的說法，超過 30 分，則用差幾分到幾點來敍述，而 after 即爲「之後」與「過」之意，to 則爲「到」之意。

可舉例 " It's ten after ten. " 爲 10 點過 10 分

　　　" It's ten to ten. " 爲差 10 分到 10 點

來說明，after 與 to 之用法差別。

♠ 練 習

(1) 可利用活動時鐘（如第一冊所準備的），由老師或指定同學撥動指針，分別練習第一冊的簡答法。與本單元所教的方式來練習辨認時間。

♠ 教學重點

after 與 to 之用法，對學生而言，比較不容易正確使用，反覆多次練習，務必要求學生能理解而能自然運用。

2-3 EXERCISE (p.15)

A. Write and draw .

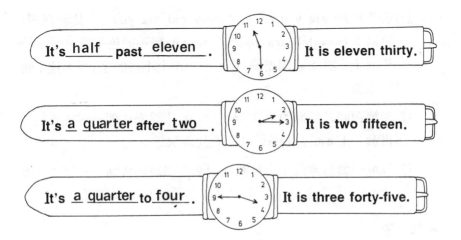

It's__half__ past__eleven__ .   It is eleven thirty.

It's _a quarter_ after__two__ .   It is two fifteen.

It's _a quarter_ to_four_ .   It is three forty-five.

B. Fill in the blanks .

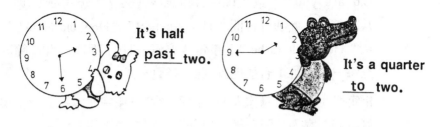

It's half __past__ two.

It's a quarter __to__ two.

Unit 3

How Old Are You?
How Tall Are You?

♠ 教學方式

(1)將" How are you？"與" How old are you？"比較練習，再將" How <u>tall</u> are you？"的 tall 用不同色筆標示並抄於黑板上，說明疑問副詞How 後，加上不同的字，所表達不同的意義。

(2)先練習回答年齡的簡答" I am 9."讓學生能練習純熟後，再教" I am 9 years old."的說法。

(3)二種句型熟悉後，方可開始對話的跟讀與背誦，可以男生當 John，女生當 Mary，分二部份並稍後可交換練習。

♠ 練 習

(1)教師可指定一學生至台前，問" How are you？"" How old are you？"或" How tall are you？"等句型，並要其回答後，教師可再問" How is he?"，"How old is he？"或" How tall is he？"等句型，讓全班練習回答，如此輪流至每一人均曾上台並能流利回答為止。

(2)指定學生回去記錄家人的年齡與身高為家庭作業，下次上課可改詢問家人（配合第一冊）之身高等作不同之練習。

♠ 教學重點

在本單元練習中，應注意避免多種句型同時練習，身高之公分與英吋的說法，可視必要再補充英吋之練習。

Uɴɪᴛ 4

There Is a Blackboard.
There Are Four Books.

♠ 教學方式

(1) 首先複習第一冊 " This is a(an)＿＿＿＿＿ ."的句型，將二種句型並列抄寫於黑板上，分別解釋與比較差別。

(2) 用 " There is a(an)＿＿＿＿＿ ."的句型來練習 p.19 之生字，或利用教室內之物品作練習。

(3) 介紹複數之說法，只將單數之 be 動詞「is」改為複數「are」即可，以同樣的物品，分別作 " There is a (an)＿＿＿＿＿ ." 與 " There are ＿＿＿＿＿ ."的比較練習。

♠ 練　習

將全班分為兩組，每次各推舉一人站起來，就所見之物說出上面練習之句型，如 " There is a pencil." " There are students."凡有錯誤或答不出來者扣一分，不可重述已提之物，記分競賽，以複習單字與熟悉句型。

♠ 教學重點

(1) 本單元第 20 頁介紹複數句型時，部份名詞的複數型，因牽涉到不規則變化如 butterflies 之去 y 加 ies，與 pencilboxes 之加 es 等，故可簡略介紹不規則名詞複數之變化，如果字尾是 y 而 y 之前面二個字母均為子音時，則必須去 y 加 ies，否則則加 s 即可如 toys，而字尾如為 s，x，sh，ch 等則加 es。

(2)關於名詞複數形後之 s 發音可能爲「s」,「z」或「ız」,
可略加說明即可。

(3)「我有一隻狗」 I <u>have</u> a dog. 之有,與「那裏有一隻狗」
There <u>is</u> a dog. 的有,用法不同,須解釋,以免學生誤
用。

習題解答

4-3 EXERCISE（p.23）

1. *There are two boys.*
   There is a girl.

2. *There is a lion.*

3. *There are three tigers.*

4. *There are ten eggs.*

5. *There is an apple.*

Is There a House?
Are There Two Dogs?

♠ 教學方式

(1) 首先複習第一冊 " This is a(an)_____ ." 變疑問句與否定句之方式，再將 " There is a(an)_____ ." 變疑問句與否定句之方式與其相同的道理告訴學生，並做練習。

(2) 利用課本上之圖片、或教室內可目見之物所問答練習，單數句型熟悉之後，再練習複數的疑問句與否定句。

♠ 練 習

要求學生回家準備一張圖卡，並熟悉圖卡上各物之名稱，下次上課帶來，交由老師分組分配或抽問作競賽練習。

5-1 LET'S PRACTICE (p.26)

1. *Is there a duck?*　　　　*Yes, there is.*

　Is there a boy?　　　　*Yes, there is.*

　Is there a hen?　　　　*No, there is not.*

　Is there a lion?　　　　*Yes, there is.*

　Is there a fish?　　　　*No, there is not.*

2. Is there a bird ?　　　　　No, there is not.

   Is there a kite ?　　　　　Yes, there is.

   Is there a girl ?　　　　　Yes, there is.

   Is there a flower ?　　　　No, there is not.

   Is there a rabbit ?　　　　Yes, there is.

3. Is there an umbrella?　　　Yes, there is.

   Is there a table ?　　　　　Yes, there is.

   Is there a cat ?　　　　　No, there is not.

   Is there a zebra?　　　　　Yes, there is.

   Is there a violin ?　　　　　Yes, there is.

4. Is there a ship?　　　　　Yes, there is.

   Is there an airplane ?　　　No, there is not.

   Is there a hot sun ?　　　　Yes, there is.

   Is there a car ?　　　　　Yes, there is.

   Is there a bird ?　　　　　Yes, there is.

5. Is there a chair ?　　　　　Yes, there is.

   Is there a door ?　　　　　Yes, there is.

   Is there a picture ?　　　　No, there is not.

   Is there a bus ?　　　　　Yes, there is.

   Is there a desk ?　　　　　Yes, there is.

5-3 EXERCISE (p. 28)

A.Look and answer.

1. Is there a bag? <u>Yes, there is</u> .

3. Are there three cats?<u>Yes, there are</u>.

2. Is there a rabbit?<u>No, there is not</u>.

4. Are there four balls?<u>Yes, there are</u>.

B.Look and draw.

1 There are two butterflies.

2 There is a bus.

3 There are six erasers.

Days and Months.

♠ 教學方式

(1)將星期與月份分成二次上課進度來敎,以免學生不易熟記,如同第一册練習數字一樣,將Sunday, Monday, ... Saturday 以韻律方式記憶背誦,直到學生均能一口氣背讀出來。

(2)練習名字之拼寫後,與學生做" What day is today ? "與" It's _____ . "之問答練習,如學生領悟力較強,可做" What day is tomorrow ? "與" What day is the day after tomorrow ? "之練習。

(3)星期練習熟悉之後,再練習月份,同樣以韻律方式將一至十二月作跟讀與記憶練習,再做" What month is it ? "與" It's _____ . "之問答練習。

♠ 練 習

可準備數張小年曆卡,將全班分爲二組,每次二位同學,分持一卡,教師隨意說一個月份,例如" March ",再說一個日子如3日,學生查看手中之年曆卡後,搶答是星期幾,先答對者得一分。

♠ 教學重點

(1)星期與月份,因爲是專有名詞,故開頭等一個字母要大寫。

⑵ 初學者，通常會依賴所默背之次序，才能說出所需之星期或
月份之說法，除了剛開始依序練習外，應多抽開作答以要求
學生能真正熟記。

 習題解答

6-3 EXERCISE (p.33)

(A) A week.

(B) A year.

Unit 7

What Is It?

♠ 教學方式

(1) 在這個單元，學到另一個疑問副詞What，如果學生年齡較大，可說明疑問詞必須放在句首，而形成疑問句，如第一冊已略為練習過的，只是生字多增加了一些範圍。

(2) 將課本上的生字，分成數組跟讀並要求學生熟記。

(3) 可指定就近一物，指定一學生問 " What is it ?"要求其回答，轉而指定另一學生，問 " Is this a _____ ?"要求其回答，如果學生對直述句改疑問句與否定句之規則不很純熟可先複習數次後，再做此連環問答的練習。

♠ 練 習

教師可準備數樣（5～10樣左右）物品，將全班分成兩組，將所有物品給全班過目，由其中一組選派一人至台前選一物（此物只有老師與同組同學方能知曉），該生將此物藏置身後，由另一組同學，就記憶中之物品作猜測，可詢問三次 " Is it a（an）_____ ?"，若皆猜不中，則換組進行，三次內猜中者，該組記一分。

7-3 EXERCISE (p.38)

A. (1) *It is a <u>chicken</u>.*

(2) *<u>It is a bee.</u>*

(3) *<u>It is a cat.</u>*

B. (1) *It is a <u>box</u>*

(2) *<u>It is a butterfly.</u>*

(3) *<u>It is a window.</u>*

Unit 8,9

These Are Pears.
Those Are Pears.

♠ 教學方式

(1) 首先複習" This is a (an)_____ ."與" That is a (an) _____ ."的句型，在複習時可適當先教本單元之部份生字於句型複習中，使學生能先練習並記憶新的生字。

(2) 將下列句型抄在黑板上

This is a book.　　　That is a book.

These are books.　　Those are books.

將 This, That, These, Those 用紅色筆標示， is, are 用另一顏色， books 之 s 再用另一種顏色，並告訴學生，單數的句子改成複數，必須①將句子中的字改成其複數。②去掉 a。

(3) 學生熟記上述二個原則後，可在黑板上寫下數個單數句子，要學生到黑板來改成複數，學生做答於黑板後，老師再領全班一起檢查 This／That 是否改爲 These／Those， is 是改成複數 are，名詞是否加上 s 或 es 成複數（規則①），與 a 是否去掉了（規則②）。以加強學生印象。

(4) Unit 9 之教法同前 Unit 7，於此不再贅述。

♠ 教學重點

在這個單元，出現名詞的複數形。對年紀稍小之學生，在此解釋不可數名詞稍難且不適合，可簡略帶過，並告訴學生，稍後會再解釋與說明。

8-3 EXERCISE (p.43)

1. *These are chickens.*

2. *Those are fish.* （注意 fish 爲不可數名詞）

3. *These are ice creams.*

4. *Those are bicycles.*

9-1 LET'S PRACTICE (p.46)

1. *What are these?*   *They're bananas.*
   What are those?   *They're pears.*

2. *What are these?*   *They're cakes.*
   What are those?   *They're sandwiches.*

3. *What are these?*   *They're eggs.*
   What are those?   *They're candy.*

4. *What are these?*   *They're pigs.*
   What are those?   *They're monkeys.*

5. *What are these?*   *They're ducks.*
   What are those?   *They're chickens.*

6. *What are these?*   *They're dogs.*
   What are those?   *They're cats.*

7. What are these?	They're pencil boxes.
What are those?	They're books.
8. What are these?	They're pencils.
What are those?	They're pens.
9. What are these?	They're vases.
What are those?	They're newspapers.

9-3 EXERCISE (p.48)

1. They are knives.

2. They are cookies.

3. They are monkeys.

4. They are watches.

Unit 10

What Is Your Father?

♠ 學習方式

(1)教師可對學生說明，用 What 問物，其意為「什麼」。如果問人，意即問其職業。

(2)練習課本上的對話，並以第 50 頁所介紹之職業替換作練習。

(3)除了課本所介紹之生字外，可實際讓學生練習問其親人之職業，增加學生練習的機會，以便學生作對答練習時，能流利地對話。

♠ 練　習

老師可與學生，或稍候讓學生與學生做，詢問彼此家人職業之對話練習。讓每位同學均有機會，練習介紹自己家人之職業。

♠ 教學重點

Who 與 What 同樣用於問人物時，易產生用法上之混淆。"Who is he?"通常是問 he 與被問者之關係，故答案可能為"He is my teacher."。如問"What is he?"則單純只是問對方之職業而已。

有時用 Who 來問人物，有意味問其 power 之意，不對此種用法，對學生而言較難理解，故可省略不提。

10-1 LET'S PRACTICE (p.51)

1. *You are a policeman.*

2. *You are a cook.*

3. *You are a nurse.*

4. *You are a teacher.*

5. *You are a doctor.*

6. *You are a sailor.*

7. *You are a farmer.*

8. *You are a typist.*

9. *You are a fireman.*

10-3 EXERCISE (p.53)

She is a typist.	*He is a fireman.*
He is a sailor.	*She is a stewardess.*

10-2 PLAY A GAME (p.52)

policeman
waitress
nurse
driver
Fireman
farmer
sailor
pilot
baker

Unit 11、12

Colors

♠ 教學方式

(1)將單元 11 所示之 7 種顏色，利用課本上之圖片或教室內所見之物作練習。老師指某物讓學生們練習回答 " This is a _____ ." 並說出此物之顏色 " It is _____ ."。

(2)學習如何發問，指出中文問某物是什麼顏色。在英文，疑問詞須置於句首，故成什麼顏色是某物 " What color is _____? "

(3)練習過以 What color 來問顏色，便可以加上單元 12 所教的新的顏色，並用 " What color is _____? " 的句型來練習問答，可由老師發問要求學生們回答，亦可由學生互相練習。

(4)解釋 or 為「或者」之意。" Is it a cat or a dog? " 意為「它是一隻貓或是一條狗？」

(5)" It is a dog. It is brown." 。我們可將上面二句，用一個句子表達。把顏色放於名詞前面來形容它，故「它是一條棕色的狗」即為 " It is a brown dog." 再加上「或者」的用法，即可開始課本 60 頁之練習。

♠ 練 習

(1)將學生分成兩組，每位同學就自己所有之物，挑選一樣收藏好。依次，每組派一人至台前，A 必須說出 B 所拿出之

物與顏色，B 亦須說出 A 所拿之物及顏色，如此反覆練習，
至每一人均曾練習止。

(2) 在黑板上列出數個生字，以下圖方式排列

cat	grass	rice
pig	TV	car
bread		

老師準備一張紙寫下顏色。
（勿讓學生看到）。

將學生分二組，先的一組可在
圖上任選一字，由老師查閱手
中顏色紙後告訴他是什麼顏色（用中文）。則被選派出來
之同學必須用一個句子表達出來，即 " It is a （顏色）
（物）." 。

習題解答

11-3 EXERCISE（p.58）

1. *This ball is purple.*   *This ball is green.*

2. *This train is blue.*   *This train is purple.*

3. *This cat is brown.*   *This cat is black.*

4. *This book is red.*   *This book is yellow.*

Unit 13.14

Sizes
Adjectives

♠ 教學方式

(1)儘管單元 13 標題爲 Sizes 。其實 13 , 14 兩單元要介紹的爲同一單元——形容詞 。首先將單元 13 之長、短、厚、薄等字作跟讀與記憶之練習 。而後視學生學習能力再加入其它形容詞 。

(2)練習某物是形容詞的句型,並解釋形容詞置於 be 動詞後,來形容主詞 ,如 p.64 之句型 。如要形成疑問句 ,則將 be 動詞置於句首即可 ,如 p.71 之句型 。

(3)形容詞置於名詞前以修飾名詞 。同中文語法「一個漂亮的(形容詞)女孩(名詞)」。

♠ 練 習

利用 13 , 14 單元所教之形容詞 ,將全班分爲兩組 ,每組準備一張紙並寫妥 3 ~ 5 樣物品之名稱 。

由其中一組先推派一人 ,至對方那組 ,抽選其中一紙條 ,然後面對自己原來的組 ,可給二個暗示 ,(但暗示中不許提及該項物品之名稱)。然後由該組自由發問 ,如 " Is it long ? ", " What color is it ? " 等 ,限時一分鐘 ,時間內答對者 ,可得一分 ,並換另一組作答 。

13-3 EXERCISE (p.68)

A. Circle the correct picture.

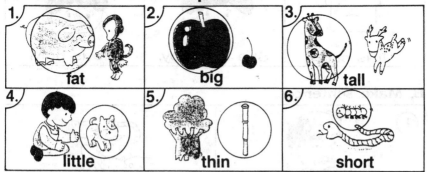

1. fat	2. big	3. tall
4. little	5. thin	6. short

B. Circle and read.

1. It is thin, thick.	2. It is long, short.
3. He is short, tall.	4. It is narrow, wide.

14-3 EXERCISE (p.73)

A. Look and draw.

| ① It is sad. | ② She is happy. | ③ He is ugly. |

B. Make sentences.

| ① He is old . | ② The cats are happy . |
| ③ She is thirsty . | ④ The robot is tall . |

LEARNING
English Readers for Children 3

Let's Start with English

Review 4

Colors, Sizes, and Adjectives

1. It is tall.
   It is new.
   It is white.

2. It is big.
   It is beautiful.
   It is yellow.

3. It is fat.
   It is dirty.
   It is pink.

4. It is wide.
   It is old.
   It is brown.

5. It is big.
   It is beautiful.
   It is red.

6. It is little.
   It is sad.
   It is green.

7. She is thin.
   She is old.
   It is gray.

8. He is fat.
   He is dirty.
   It is blue.

Where Is the Chicken?

♠ **教學方式**

(1) 利用實際物體的位置，清楚地解釋 "on,""in,""under," 及 "by" 四個字的意思。

(2) 解釋以上四字在句子中的位置。

$$主詞＋Be\text{-}動詞＋\begin{Bmatrix} on \\ in \\ under \\ by \end{Bmatrix}＋名詞$$

Example: The dog is under the table.

(3) (1)及(2)稍有概念後，由教師先示範讀出一物體的位置。讀出此物體位置時，遇到 "on,""in,""under," 或是 "by" 時，應特別大聲讀出並強調，使學生加強記憶。

♠ **練 習**

(1) 由教師將一物體（例如：鉛筆）放於桌上（或其他知道之家具上，下，裏面，或旁邊）。首先由教師將此二樣物體的名字念出再念出整個句子，但遇到要講出物體位置時，故意把口氣放慢讓學生答出物體之位置。（可一位，一位地問。）

(2) 把學生分為兩組，每組派出一位代表將所學過之東西選一樣出來並將此東西放於一位置請另一組之小朋友將此東西之位置用完整的句子講出來。如果完全答對，答對之那一組可得

一分。然後再由另一組選派另一代表出來重複此競賽，一直
到每位小朋友都出來過為止。答錯之那組不得分，再由別組
派出之代表讀出東西位置。

♠ **教學重點**

(1) 主詞及名詞前之冠詞 "the" 之定義及用法必須向學生們解釋
　清楚。不可用 "a" 或 "an" 來替代 "the"。

(2) "in" 及 "on" 兩字因拼法相近，學生較易將意思混淆在一起。
　教師應讓學生多練習此 2 字之用法，讓學生從靈活運用中學
　習及加強此 2 字之意思。切勿不可指使學生死背。

習題解答

1-1 LET'S PRACTICE (p.7)

1. *Her father and mother are in the house.*

2. *The car is by the house.*

3. *The chair is under the tree.*

4. *Her cat is in the tree.*

5. *The apple is on the chair.*

6. *The dog is in the car.*

7. *Her brother is in the tree.*

1-3 EXERCISE (p.9)

Draw and write.

Draw the ball	Draw the apple
on the table.	**in the fish.**
The ball is on the table.	The apple is in the fish.
under the desk.	**by the clock.**
The ball is under the desk.	The apple is by the clock.

The Man is at the Top of the Tree.

♠ 教學方式

(1) 由教師帶領學生們大聲讀出 "at the top of," "in the middle of," "at the bottom of," "at the side of," "in front of", "behind" 及 "near"，並糾正學生發音至每位學生都能正確發出為止。

(2) 等學生對以上之生字發音沒問題時，教師可利用 Unit 1 之教學方式，先解釋 "near" 的意思及用法，由較容易的先解釋再進級到較難的，一個一個的慢慢講解及應用，直到學生能靈活運用時再進行至下一句。

♠ 練 習

(1) 可重複 Unit 1 之遊戲，等學生們對這幾個字練習得差不多時，可加入 Unit 1 所教之 "on," "in," "under" 及 "by" 以增加學生思考能力。

(2) 教師可準備圖卡讓學生說出圖卡上東西之位置。每張圖卡說完一遍後分發給每位學生一張。點到名字之學生須將其手上之圖卡上各樣東西之位置講出來，說對者可坐下。不對者請老師將其手上之圖卡解釋給他們聽，並請學生大聲跟著老師念一次，念完後請老師再問一次可由全班同學一起回答，答後可坐下。

(3)將學生分成2組，每組每次派不同之代表至黑板畫教師所念之句子內容。先畫出及畫對者之那組可得一分。如2組都不會時，教師再上台畫圖並解釋。得分最多之那組爲優勝。

♠ 教學重點

(1)因此課所教之東西較多，教師切不可心急。應慢慢有耐心地教。

(2)注意解釋爲何有的片語用"in,"有的用"at"及爲何"near"前不加"in" or "at"時應簡潔扼要。切勿扯得太多以免弄巧成拙。

習題解答

2-1 LET'S PRACTICE (p.12)

1. *The boat is on the water.*

2. *The kite is at the bottom of (or near) the tree.*

3. *The dog is behind the car.*

4. *The book is near the table.*

5. *The duck is at the side of the house.*

6. *The eraser is by the blackboard.*

7. *The bird is at the top of the umbrella.*

8. *The bag is under the chair.*

2-3 EXERCISE (p.14)

Look and draw.

①	**Draw a bird at the top of the umbrella.**	
②	**Draw a turtle behind the girl.**	
③	**Draw a mouse at the bottom of the tree.**	
④	**Draw a ball near the table.**	
⑤	**Draw a hat at the side of the box.**	

3

Imperatives (1)

♠ 教學方式

(1) 教師從最常用之 "stand up" 及 "sit down" 開始教。教時
應一面大聲唸出一面利用手勢及動作使學生了解其意思。等
學生了解後,再利用同種方法幫助學生學習 "come,""go,"
"write,""open,""jump,""walk,""run,""catch" 及
"throw" 等字。

(2) 學生了解了差不多時,可請三、五位小朋友至台前表演動作。
由全體小朋友將所學過之字再重新複習一次,並由老師在旁
指導及糾正發音。

(3) 由教師解釋祈使詞(imperatives)之用法及其在句子中之
位置。讓學生有個概念即可,不必太深入講解。

♠ 練 習

(1) 將學生分為 2 組,每組利用輪流方式,每次派一人出場聽老
師指令行事。如老師說 "Go to the door." 每組所派之學
生必須按照教師之命令做事。做對者之那組可得一分否則不
給分。直到每位小朋友皆輪過後遊戲才停止。得分最高之那
組為優勝。

(2) 讓全體小朋友一起聽從教師所說之句子做動作。(也可請小
朋友一位、一位地輪流上台說口令讓其他小朋友照他所說去

做 。）口令可一直說，越說越快直到沒有小朋友做錯為止。每次做錯之學生另編成二或三組，由所有口令都做對之小朋友指揮發號口令。口令做錯者淘汰直到 20 句口令全發號完了，剩下最多人數之那組為優勝。

(3)可利用 " Simon says" 或其他加在口令前之口號以增加趣味性及反應能力。加在口令前之口號可為 " Father says" 。

♠ **教學重點**

(1)請教師多強調 "come" 及 "go" 這 2 字的意思。學生常會將此 2 字混淆在一起而導致句子與原要說之句子的意思不合或因一時之疏忽而將此 2 字用錯地方。

(2)教師應每堂課前重複練習本課之詞句以加深學生印象。最基本之 "stand up" 及 "sit down" 一定要求每位學生都會。

習題解答

3-1 LET'S PRACTICE (p.17)

1. *Stand up.*

2. *Sit down.*

3. *Jump.*

4. *Run.*

5. *Turn around.*

6. *Write a letter.*

7. *Throw a ball.*

8. *Catch a ball.*

3-3 EXERCISE (p.19)

A. Look and circle.

B. Look and draw.

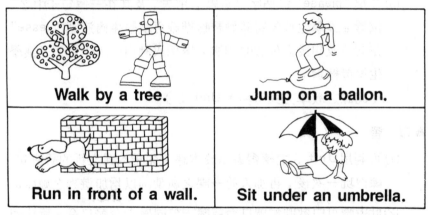

Walk by a tree.

Jump on a ballon.

Run in front of a wall.

Sit under an umbrella.

4

Imperatives (2)

♠教學方式

(1)利用手勢及動作解釋本課之祈使詞。由最簡單容易記的到較難之詞。

(2)反覆練習讓學生做動作及大聲讀出每一個祈使詞使其加深記憶。

(3)介紹"please"這個字之意思，用法，及其在一個句子中之位置。讓學生首先將其發音唸準確再讓學生們適應"please"在句前及句後之位置的用法。舉例或利用課本上之例子讓學生反覆練習。

（此課之教學方式可參考 Unit 3）

♠練習

(1)可利用 Unit 3 之練習遊戲於本課。先把本課之新的祈使句練習玩一次後，再加入前一課之祈使詞以增加遊戲之難度。

(2)此遊戲可由教師發號口令或請一位同學上台發口令。玩法如下：如施放口令者說出"please"時，全班同學才可照著口令的指示做動作。如發口令者並沒說"please"時，不可照著指示做。做錯者淘汰。最後剩下之三位同學爲優勝者。可將"please"的位置改變（有時在句前，有時在句後）藉以增加學生之聽力及提高其注意力。

(3)由教師製作多張圖卡，上註明一祈使詞後發給每位小朋友。發圖卡時，有祈使詞之那面朝下並告訴學生不可偷看。點到名字之學生需起立，將圖卡上之祈使詞大聲唸出。唸完後利用那一祈使詞造一個句子並示範所造句子之動作。遇到不會之小朋友請教師從旁指導並請其它小朋友注意聽。

♠ 教學重點

儘量讓學生從動作及遊戲中，直接學習本課祈使詞之意思。不可叫學生利用死背之方法將他們死記起來。

習題解答

4-3 EXERCISE (p.24)

A. 1. <u>Shut</u> (or <u>Close</u>) your book.

2. <u>Touch</u> your nose.

3. <u>Push</u> your chair.

4. <u>Raise</u> your hand.

B.

1. Write / Draw a circle.
2. Pick up / Hold up a pencil.
3. Shut / Open a window.
4. Push / Pull a desk.

What Are You Doing?

♠ 教學方式

(1) 由教師先介紹及利用動作解釋本課之生字：“eating,” “sleeping” 及 “singing” 等。教師然後帶領學生大聲唸本課之生字一遍。一面唸一面做動作並要求學生一起做。

(2) 介紹最基本之現在進行式 “I am ~ing.” 講解現在進行式時應以簡潔扼要為主。如遇到學生問及為何在動詞後面需加上 -ing 時，應解釋為英文文法裏之一規則。就像為什麼在母音開頭之名詞前冠詞用 “an”，而遇到子音開頭時用 “a” 之原因一樣。千萬不可不解釋而令學生死背。

(3) 等學生將 “I am ~ing.” 能靈活運用時再介紹問句之問法。以下為 2 種可使用之問法及回答：

　A) What are you doing?

　　→ I am ~ing.

　B) Are you ~ing?

　　→ Yes, I am.

　　→ No, I am not. I am ~ing.

♠ 練 習

(1) 由教師做一學過之動作利用輪流方式請學生一次一個地站起來用 “Are you ~ing?” 發問。如果猜對則教師說 “Yes, I am ~ing.” 後立刻換另一動作請下一位學生發問，直到每位小朋友都輪過為止。如果學生猜錯時，教師則說 "No, I am not ～ing"後，由同一位學生繼續發問，一共可發問三次，如三次都未猜中則第4次發問時改為 "What are you doing?"教師則必須將答案講出來。此遊戲也可請一同學擔任表演動作之角色或可由每位同學輪流擔任。

(2)由教師準備足夠全班同學人數之圖卡，上標明～ing。一次由一同學上台抽一圖卡（不能讓其他同學看到），看完後表演圖卡上之動作。首先將全體學生分為甲、乙兩組，然後再由各組以舉手方式發問，先舉手之那組可先發問。（利用練習(1)之方式發問。）如果猜對則可得一分，再由下一位同學上台抽圖卡表演。如果不對則把發問機會讓給另一組之小朋友直至猜對為止。教師可將以前學過可表演出來之動詞一併列入。

♠ 教學重點

(1)現在進行式之動詞必須加上 -ing，請教師務必將此觀念正確地輸入學生記憶中。

(2)現在進行式之基本句型也應讓學生有個概念：

主詞＋Be 動詞＋動詞 -ing.　　→敍述句

Be 動詞＋主詞＋動詞 -ing?　　→問句

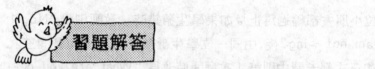

5-3 EXERCISE（p. 29）

I am jumping.	I am eating.	I am walking.
I am sleeping.	I am running.	I am sitting.
I am singing.	I am writing.	I am reading.

What Is She Doing?

♠ 教學方式

(1)先由教師將本課之生字帶領學生們大聲讀出，讀出時應配合動作，使學生由動作中了解字的意思。讓學生們熟讀本課之生字及充分了解其意思後，教師再加入已學過之現在進行式之動詞，讓學生們也大聲讀一遍。

(2)學生們能自己讀出所有本課之現在進行式動詞後，再介紹本課之基本句型：

A) What is (s)he ~ing?

　　→ (S)he is ~ing.

　　or (S)he is ~ing a(n) ＿＿＿＿＿.

　　or (S)he is ~ing his/her ＿＿＿＿＿.

B) Is (s)he ~ing?

　　→ Yes, (s)he is ~ing.

　　→ No, (s)he is not ~ing.

　　　(S)he is ~ing.

(3)儘可能利用手勢及動作。一面讀出句子一面做動作，使學生從動作中了解句子的意思，而不是單從中文解釋方面了解一句子的意義。

♠ 練 習

(1)可依照 Unit 5 之遊戲方法利用於本課中。可加入已學過之
東西應用於問答題。例如：由同學A表演正在讀一本書，搶
答或回答之同學應將書也一起說出來。不可只說學生A為
"(S)he is reading." 應為 "(S)he is reading a book."
現在式之動詞及其後之名詞兩者都說對者才給分。

(2)將全體學生分為三人一組。由每組派二人出來（採用輪流方
式）到教師那兒去抽圖卡，看完圖卡後交還給老師（不可告
訴同組之那一位小朋友圖卡的內容），立刻跑回自己的那組
由二位看到圖卡之其中一位表演圖卡上所看到之圖案，只能
用比的不能用口說，而由另一位看到圖卡者在旁回答未看到
圖卡的那位同學的問題。當開始表演時，未看到圖卡之那位
同學應問 " Is (s)he ～ing?" 如果是的話，回答者應回答
"Yes, (s)he is ～ing." 再另派二位出來到老師那兒抽圖卡
重覆此遊戲，直到每組的小朋友皆表演過動作為止。每位小
朋友只能擔任同一種角色一次，也就是說每組之每位小朋友
應當表演者一次，回答者一次，及問問題者一次。如果問問
題之那位同學猜錯時，則回答 "No, (s)he is not ～ing."
並給予問的那位同學再2次機會發問。如第三次仍猜不中則
由回答之那位同學將 "No, (s)he is not ～ing. (S)he is
～ing." 說出來。遇到說 "(S)he is ～ing." 的時候應大聲
說出。每位小朋友皆擔任過三種不同角色而第一個表演完之
那組，獲得優勝。

♠ **教學重點**

現在進行式：

A）敍述句：

主詞	Be動詞	現在進行式動詞	名　　詞
I YOU HE SHE	ARE AM IS	～ing	a(n)＿＿ ; my＿＿ a(n)＿＿ ; your＿＿ a(n)＿＿ ; his ＿＿ a(n)＿＿ ; her ＿＿

B）疑問句：

將 Be 動詞移到主詞之前。

習題解答

6-1 LET'S PRACTICE （p.32）

1. *He is running.*　　2. *He is singing.*

3. *He is swimming.*　　4. *She is sleeping.*

5. *She is cooking.*　　6. *She is walking.*

7. *He is drinking.*　　8. *He is eating.*

6-3 EXERCISE (p.34)

Circle and read.

1. (He) is clapping. / She (singing)
2. He is (cooking). / (She) washing.
3. (He) is shouting. / She (crying).
4. He is (cooking). / (She) (washing).
5. (He) is eating. / She (drinking).
6. (He) is (pulling) a desk. / She pushing
7. He is (playing) a violin. / (She) singing
8. (He) is (throwing) a ball. / She catching

7

My Daily Life

♠ 教學方式

(1) 先由教師領全班學生一面看課本上之圖一面大聲唸出在圖旁邊之句子。唸完後請全體學生們一起唸，由教師在旁糾正發音並使學生由圖了解其句子的意思。

(2) 介紹並解釋句子的構造。 主詞＋動詞＋名詞＋時間。

(3) 學生了解以上二點後，再由教師舉出一些常可用到之問句。例如：

    A）What do you do at ＿＿＿＿＿？

    B）Do you ＿＿＿＿＿？

    C）What time do you ＿＿＿＿＿？

    並請教師講解應如何回答以上之問句。

♠ 練 習

(1) 請每位小學生一個一個輪流上台向全班同學報告，一天中他平常都做了些什麼事。也可請有問題之小朋友，利用老師教過之問句問在台上的那位同學。

(2) 由老師準備數張上有各種時間之卡片再分發給每位學生。點到名字之同學需將卡片上之時間先唸出，再說出在這時間他通常都在做什麼。

♠ **教學重點**

　(1)將一句子改爲問句時（在本課中）因主詞爲 "you"，助動
　　詞應爲 "do"。解釋用助動詞 "do" 把一句子改爲問句時，
　　其在句中的位置及意義。例如：

　　　I come home at six o'clock.
　　　→ Do you come home at six o'clock?

　(2)應強調 "時間" 在句中的位置。

7-1 LET'S PRACTICE (p. 37)

1. *I get up in the morning.*

2. *I wash my face.*　　　3. *I eat my breakfast.*

4. *I go to school.*　　　5. *I study at school.*

6. *I play baseball.*　　　7. *I watch TV.*

8. *I do my homework.*　　9. *I go to bed.*

7-3 EXERCISE (p. 39)

　　*I get up at six o'clock and eat my breakfast at
seven o'clock. I go to school at seven twenty. I
come home at five o'clock. I do my homework at
six thirty and watch TV at eight o'clock. I go
to bed at nine o'clock.*

（此大題可讓學生儘量發揮，以上僅供參考。）

8

What Do You Have for Breakfast?

♠ 教學方式

(1)首先由教師將 "breakfast" 的中文字面意思解釋給學生，然後反問學生早餐時他們平常都吃些什麼。將所學過之早餐食物名稱全寫在黑板上。再由教師將本課之早餐食物名稱也一併寫在黑板上，並帶領學生把所有在黑板的字唸一次，一面唸一面解釋其中文意思或利用圖畫解釋至學生們能朗朗上口為止。

(2)複習 Unit 7 之助動詞 "do" 在問句中的用法。並將 "for" 在本課之意思解釋出來利用舉例之方法。讓學生從多種句型或句子中了解 "for" 的意思。以上學生明白後再介紹本課之主要問句 "What do you have for breakfast/lunch/dinner？"

(3)利用本課之主要問句及 "do" 開頭之相關句子，配合在黑板上之食物名稱反覆讓學生做問答練習。到學生對助動詞 "do" 開頭之句子能靈活運用時，加入本課另外的一些生字做同樣之練習。

♠ 練 習

(1)每位學生以輪流方式到台上做一段一分鐘的演講。內容包括一天三餐平常都吃些什麼及在學校裏都上那些課。

(2) 首先由教師準備些畫有所學過食物之圖卡，再將全班分為
　　 A、B 兩組。將圖卡平均分配放置於每組之前的桌子上。由
　　每組每次以輪流方式，由一位學生到組前之桌上拿起一張圖
　　卡並利用圖卡上之圖畫造一句子。句子造對者方可回到原來
　　的位置，而下一位輪到的小朋友才可出來到桌上抽圖卡並做
　　同樣的事情。接下去皆以此類推。句子造錯者有三次機會可
　　重造句子，如三次皆錯時由教師在旁協助指導，並要求此位
　　小朋友唸三次教師所教之句子，才可換下位小朋友上前抽圖
　　卡。最先輪完的那組為優勝。

♠ **教學重點**

　　有些小朋友可能會對助動詞 "do" 的意思及為何改成問句時要
將 "do" 放置於主詞前，遇到此問題應儘量簡單解釋過去，切
勿過分深入解釋而導入學生混淆不清。

習題解答

8-3 EXERCISE (p.44)

B. 1. *Yes, I do.　I get up at six.*

2. *Yes, I do.　I brush my teeth and wash my face.*

3. *Yes, I do.　I have milk and bread for breakfast.*

4. *Yes, I do.　I go to school at seven thirty.*

5. *Yes, I do.　I have six classes.*

6. *Yes, I do.　I come home at four o'clock.*

7. *Yes, I do.   I watch TV.*

8. *Yes, I do.   I do my homework.*

9. *Yes, I do.   I go to bed at nine o'clock.*

以上如爲否定句時，句型爲

　　No, I don't. I ～.

Do You Have a Hat?

♠ 教學方式

(1) 將本課所有的名詞畫在圖卡上，利用圖卡解釋本課生字的意
思。帶領學生一面讀一面看圖使其了解所有名詞的意思並糾
正發音，至每位小朋友都能看到圖而說出其英文名字爲止。

(2) 利用本課生字及基本問句 "Do you have a(n) ～?" 及
"Who has a(n) ～?" 互相配合練習問答問題。

♠ 練 習

(1) 由教師將已準備好的圖卡一張一張地拿給學生們看，並利用
本課之基本問句問學生，由點到之學生回答教師的問題，直
到每位小朋友皆輪過爲止。

(2) 教師將全班學生分爲幾小組。每位學生手上必須持有一學過
之東西。首先每組以輪流方式每次派一人出來當發問者。發
問者可用本課所學過之問句問同組之同學 "Do you have
a(n) ～?", "Does (s)he have a(n) ～?" 及 " Who has
a(n) ～?" 等。被問到之同學必須回答，如回答不出則換他
當發問者。如每位同學皆會回答，則以輪流方式派人當發問
者。發問者未發問前，同組之同學應介紹他手上有什麼東西
"I have a(n) ～." 同組之同學皆介紹過後才開始發問。教
師可將此遊戲訂爲15～20分鐘。當時間到時，每組的發問
者必須到台前表演唱歌或跳舞等。

♠ **教學重點**

(1) 助動詞

主　　格	助動詞
第一，二人稱單，複數 I，YOU，WE 第三人稱複數 THEY	DO
第三人稱單數 HE，SHE，IT	DOES

(2) 問句之回答：

　　A）Do ～ have a(n)～？

　　　→ Yes, ～ do.　No, ～ don't.

　　B）Does ～ have a(n)～？

　　　→ Yes, ～ does.　No, ～ doesn't.

　　C）Who has a(n)～？

　　　→～ has.　or ～ and ～ have.

　　　（二人或二人以上用 "have"）

(3) 在助動詞後面之動詞 " 有 " 皆為 "have"。教師應強調此點。

習題解答

9-3 EXERCISE （p.49）

　A. *I have an umbrella.*　　*You have a baby.*

　　He has a horse.　　　　*She has a dog.*

Does Your Mother Cook Breakfast?

♠ 教學方式

(1)教師可利用圖卡及手勢動作，一面帶領全體學生讀出本課之生字一面解釋其意思。糾正學生發音至朗朗上口為止。

(2)介紹本課之基本問句" What does (s)he ～?"及" Does (s)he ～?"與應如何回答。讓學生配合本課生字靈活運用練習回答。

♠ 練 習

(1)可加入前幾課之問句配合此課之問句，以輪流或點名方式利用書上之圖書或圖卡加強學生練習問答。教師也可請一學生上台代替教師的位置問全班同學問題。

(2)讓學生一個個上台講一段平常他家人都做些什麼事。例如：他媽媽一天的生活是如何的呢？他弟弟、哥哥、姊姊，或妹妹呢？爸爸呢？

♠ 教學重點

第三人稱單數動詞一定要加 -s（普通的動詞都加 -s ）。除了 -s, -ch, 及 -sh 字母 ending 加 -es 外，其餘之第三人稱單數現在式動詞都加 -s，此點應讓學生有個基本概念，並要求其在家或在校多加練習。

習題解答

10-1 LET'S PRACTICE (p.52)

				⁴w	r	i	t	e	s
				a					
	¹s		s	t	u	²d	i	³e	s
	i		h			r		a	
⁵d	a	n	c	e	s	i		t	
	g		s			n		s	
	s					k			
		⁶c	o	o	k	s			

10-3 EXERCISE (p.54)

B. 1. *No, he doesn't. He comes home at four o'clock.*

2. *Yes, he plays baseball.*

3. *Yes, he has dinner at six.*

4. *No, he doesn't. He does his homework at seven o'clock.*

5. *No, he doesn't. He watches TV.*

6. *No, he doesn't. He goes to bed at nine thirty.*

What Do You Like?

♠ 教學方式

(1)將本課之生字用圖卡方式畫出。然後利用圖卡說明一東西之英文名字，要求學生們大聲唸出並糾正其發音。直至學生們能熟讀爲止。

(2)解釋 "like" 爲 " 喜歡 " 。利用圖卡造 " I like ～." 及 " I don't like ～." 等句子。讓每位學生皆能運用此二句及圖卡靈活造句爲止。

(3)介紹本課之基本問句 " What do you like？" 及 " Do you like ～？" ，讓學生練習問答。

♠ 練 習

(1)教師可利用本課之基本問句，以點名方式問每位學生。如遇到學生不懂問什麼時，再將圖卡拿出並把講話速度放慢。再不懂時，則請教師從旁指導。教師可加入前幾課與本課略有關係之句子，生字，或問句來問學生。一方面加強其思考及應變能力，一方面複習。

(2)請學生在家準備一套與教師相同之圖卡帶到學校。然後二個二個或更多人一組，互相利用圖卡發問同組之小朋友。由教師在旁指導。

♠ 教學重點

　(1)"Do you like～?"之～一定是複數，除非是不可數名詞或
　　　指定爲某種東西時。教師應强調此點。

　(2)教師應解釋如 "meat," "coffee" 等爲不可數名詞，並把不
　　　可數名詞及可數名詞之不同處，講解給學生聽使其了解。

習題解答

11-3 EXERCISE（p.59）

Susan and _Mark_ like coffee.

Mary and _Susan_ don't like soup.

Mary and _John_ like ice cream.

John and _Susan_ don't like tea.

John and _Mark_ like soup.

Mary and _John_ don't like coffee.

 12

What Can You Do?

♠ 教學方式

(1)將 "can" 及 "cannot" 之中文意思解釋出來。然後由本課之生字中，從較容易之動作利用手勢或姿勢動作表示出意思，並大聲將此動作之英文名稱唸出，請學生跟著教師一起做。再由教師教到較難的動作利用同種方法。

(2)講解 "I can ～." 及 "I cannot ～." 時配合本課之動詞，利用動作或手勢使學生從表演中，領悟出句子的意思。教師也可利用書中之圖畫或圖卡，造各樣不同之 "can" 或 "cannot" 之句子，讓學生由多方面學習這二個字。要求學生跟教師一起說及做動作。

(3)介紹利用 "can" 可造出之問句，例如 "Can ～～?","What can ～～? " 等。利用這些問句與學生練習問答。

♠ 練 習

(1) 利用已準備好之圖卡和本課教過之問句，要求學生自己問自己答，或由老師問學生答，或者也可請一學生問則另一學生答。

(2)請全班學生排成二行面向黑板。由第一行第一位學生說出一動物名稱，東西，或人名後蹲下，由第二位學生說出一動詞後也蹲下，然後由第三位小朋友將第一及第二位小朋友所說之字用 "can" 或 "cannot" 造句說出來。說對者才可蹲下，不對者則需重新從最後一位開始排。以後以此類推。教師可每30秒喊停一次。輪到正要說之那位小朋友則需上台表演。

♠ 教學重點

"can" 後面之動詞永遠是原形動詞，不管主詞是否是第三人稱單數。

習題解答

12-1 LET'S PRACTICE（p.62）

1. *It's number five.*

2. *I can see a woman in the house.*

3. *She is standing at the window.*

4. *I can see a boy in the yard.*

5. *He is standing under a tree.*

6. *Yes, I can see a dog. It is in the tree.*

12-3 EXERCISE（p.64）

1. *Yes, I can cook.*

2. *No, I cannot fly.*

3. *No, I cannot eat five bananas.*

4. *Yes, I can write.*

5. *No, it cannot jump.*

6. *No, it cannot swim.*

第 三 冊 學 習 內 容 一 覽 表

單元	內　容	練　習	活　動	習　作
複習第二冊	1.問候語、年齡、身高、星期和月份 2.有沒有～? 3.它是什麼(他、她做什麼)?這些(那些)是什麼? 4.顏色，大小和形容詞	Do and say. Point and say. Look and say. Question and answer.		
1	小雞在那裏?	Read and answer：從短文及插圖中練習 in, on, under, by 的用法	歌曲：Pussy cat, pussy cat	Draw and write.
2	這人在樹的頂端	Look and answer：從圖中練習 in front, behind, in the middle, near 的問與答	遊戲：Three in a row.	Look and draw.
3	命令(1)	Look and say：從例圖中來練習各種命令動作的說法	遊戲：Captain says ……	Look and circle. Look and draw.
4	命令(2)	Say and do：從實際的活動中練習各種命令句的說法		
5	你正在做什麼?	Do and say：從實際動作中練習 Are you～ing? 的問答	歌曲：Are you sleeping?	Look and say.
6	她正在做什麼?	Question and answer：作 What is he / she doing? 的問答練習	遊戲：Hat game.	Circle and read.
7	我的一天生活	Look and say：從各圖中練習日常生活習慣動作的說法	遊戲：Say and do.	Make a story.
8	你早餐吃些什麼?	Question and answer：練習 Do you have～for breakfast? 的問答	遊戲：Do and say.	Read and write.
9	你有一頂帽子嗎?	Ask and answer：從所給的圖中練習 have ～與 has 的問答	遊戲：Guessing game.	Trace and write. Read and color.
10	你的母親作早餐嗎?	Write and say：從圖中作縱橫字謎以及 Does he / she～? 的問答	歌曲：Rain, rain, go away	Read and answer.
11	你喜歡什麼?	Circle and say：以自己的情況來說 I like ～. I don't like ～.	遊戲：Do you like your neighbors?	Look, write and read.
12	你能做些什麼?	Read and answer：從一段短文及圖中作 can ～ 的問答練習	遊戲：I can swim.	Look and write.
複習	看圖練習 看圖練習 看圖練習 看圖練習 看圖練習 看圖練習 生字總復習	Look and write. Point and say. Read a story. Look and say. Say and do. Free Composition. Picture dictionary.		

LEARNING
English Readers for Children 4

Let's Start with English

Review 2 Present Progressive Tense

 習題解答 （p.2）

3. A : Is he cooking?
   B : No, he isn't.
   He isn't cooking.

   A : What is he doing?
   B : He is washing.

   A : What is he washing?
   B : He is washing his car.

4. A : Is he sleeping?
   B : No, he isn't.
   He isn't sleeping.

   A : What is he doing?
   B : He is reading.

   A : What is he reading?
   B : He is reading the
   newspaper.

5. A : Are they reading?
   B : No, they aren't.
   They aren't reading.

   A : What are they doing?
   B : They are drinking.

   A : What are they drinking?
   B : They are drinking
   water.

6. A : Is he drinking?
   B : No, he isn't.
   He isn't drinking.

   A : What is he doing?
   B : He is writing.

   A : What is he writing?
   B : He is writing a letter.

7. A : Is she swimming?
   B : No, she isn't.
   　　She isn't swimming.

   A : What is she doing?
   B : She is washing.

   A : What is she washing?
   B : She is washing clothes.

8. A : Is he shouting?
   B : No, he isn't.
   　　He isn't shouting.

   A : What is he doing?
   B : He is watching.

   A : What is he watching?
   B : He is watching TV.

9. A : Is she flying?
   B : No, she isn't.
   　　She isn't flying.

   A : What is she doing?
   B : She is playing.

   A : What is she playing?
   B : She is playing the
   　　violin.

10. A : Is he running?
    B : No, he isn't.
    　　He isn't running.

    A : What is he doing?
    B : He is playing.

    A : What is he playing?
    B : He is playing baseball.

11. A : Is she clapping?
    B : No, she isn't.
    　　She isn't clapping.

    A : What is she doing?
    B : She is singing.

    A : What is she singing?
    B : She is singing a
    　　song.

12. A : Is she washing?
    B : No, she isn't.
    　　She isn't washing.

    A : What is she doing?
    B : She is cooking.

    A : What is she cooking?
    B : She is cooking dinner.

Unit 1

MY SCHOOL

♠ 學習目標

複習 " how many " 及 " there are " 的句型並學習序數的運用。

♠ 教學方式

(1) 老師先將下列句子寫在黑板上：

How many days are there in a week?
There are seven days in a week.

How many students are there in the classroom?
There are ten students in the classroom.

帶小朋友跟讀，複習 " How many ～ " 及 " There are ～ "
的句型，直到他們朗朗上口為止。高年級的小朋友，可以
讓他們用學過的單字嘗試自己造句，並將句子寫在黑板上。

(2) 在黑板上寫出如下的 1 — 7 數字與序數，告訴小朋友「第
一、第二……」的概念。並帶讀，糾正發音及語調。

one	the first
⟨	⟨
seven	the seventh

♠ 教學重點

(1) 除了第一、二、三，及五之外，絕大多數的序數都是在原
基數之後加上 th，唸 /θ/，注意不要發成 /s/。又序數之
前要加定冠詞 the。

(2)序數是新的內容，故本課只先教「第一」到「第七」。

♠ **練 習**

(1)將小朋友分成2人一組，回家將課文對話部分作演練，下次
上課時，讓每組出來做角色扮演，表現優異的小朋友，可給
予獎勵。

(2)老師準備好7張卡片，上面分別用中文寫上「星期日」到「
星期六」，再將卡片蓋起來，隨意放在桌上，讓每個小朋友
上台來輪流抽，利用抽到的卡片來造句，如抽到「星期二」
的小朋友，必須大聲說出" Tuesday is the third day of
the week ."回答不出來的小朋友，老師可從旁指導，並讓
全班小朋友跟著唸三次。

習題解答

1-1 LET'S PRACTICE （p.8）

1. A : *How many apples are there on the table ?*
   B : *There are six apples on the table.*

2. A : *How many cats are there under the desk ?*
   B : *There are three cats under the table.*

3. A : *How many birds are there in the tree ?*
   B : *There are four birds in the tree.*

4. A : *How many chairs are there by the window ?*
   B : *There are two chairs by the window.*

*   *   *

1. *Monday is the second day of the week.*

2. *Tuesday is the third day of the week.*

3. *Wednesday is the fourth day of the week.*

4. *Thursday is the fifth day of the week.*

5. *Friday is the sixth day of the week.*

6. *Saturday is the seventh day of the week.*

1·3 EXERCISE （p.10）

Where are you going?

I am going to school.

What grade are you in?

I'm in the fourth grade.

What grade are you in?

Draw yourself here.

I'm in the fifth grade.

What time is your first class?

It starts at eight o'clock.

How many students are there in your class?

There are twelve students in my class.

Unit 2

HAPPY BIRTHDAY TO YOU

♠ 教學目標

讓孩子能用英文表達日期，為上一課序數的延伸。

♠ 教學方式

(1) 老師先將十二個月份的英文複習一遍，利用抽問的方式，讓小朋友看到中文能立即反應唸出。

(2) 將 one 到 thirty-one 寫在黑板上或利用課本的月曆，告訴小朋友，如何將數字變成序數，讓他們自己從家裏帶一張月曆來，在上面用英文寫上 1 到 31 的序數。

(3) 介紹本課句型：

My birthday is on ＋月份＋序數。

(4) 除了生日以外，也可利用國定假日或著名的節慶來引導小朋友練習日期的說法。

♠ 教學重點

(1) 在日期之前要加上 on，應提醒小朋友不要漏掉了。

(2) 將數字改為序數的規則是字尾加 th，但特別注意 " eighth "、" ninth "、" twelfth "、" twentieth "、" thirtieth " 這些字有例外。

♠ 練 習

(1) 老師發給每位小朋友一張紙，讓他們用中文寫上自己的生日，用手拿著。老師再用點名或輪流的方式，叫一位小朋友出來，先問他，"When is your birthday？"，小朋友回答之後，老師再隨便指另一個小朋友問他，"When is his（her）birthday？"；回答正確之後，才可以回座。如此一直到每位小服友都出來過爲止。

(2) 將小朋友分爲兩組，老師在黑板上寫出日期，先舉手回答正確的一組得分。最終積分多者爲優勝。

習題解答　　2-3　EXERCISE　（p.15）

Look and write.

The Birthdays of My Family Members

　　My father's birthday is on December first. My mother's birthday is on March fifteenth. My brother's birthday is on August twenty-second. My sister's birthday is on January thirtieth. And my birthday is on September nineteenth.

Do you know these dates？

A : What day is it today？

B : *It is Friday today.*

A : What date is it today？

B : *It is May eighteenth.*

1. *December twenty-fifth*
2. *October tenth*
3. *April fourth*
4. *March eighth*
5. *March twelfth*
6. *August eighth*

Unit 3

HIM AND HER

♠ 學習目標

如何使用代名詞的受格，如 them，us，me，him，her。

♠ 教學方式

(1) 將 " I like Mary." 寫在黑板上，講解「主詞＋動詞＋受詞」的句型，可適時讓小朋友自己用這個公式來造句，並寫在黑板上。將重點放在受詞上。

(2) 將原句 " I like Mary "（我喜歡瑪麗。）改爲 " I like her."（我喜歡她。）告訴小朋友受詞的「她」，不可用 she，而應用 she 的受格 her。並在黑板上寫上：

she → her　　he → him　　they → them
you → you　　I → me　　we → us

帶小朋友跟讀，讓他們朗朗上口爲止。

(3) 將黑板上的 her，him，them，us，me，you 等受格擦掉，點名請每個小朋友出來，將老師所指的代名詞的受格唸出來，如老師指 " she "，小朋友則回答受格 " her "。直到他們能立即反應爲止。

(4) 請小朋友上台來將所有的句子，改爲有受格 her，him 等的句子。再由老師帶讀。

♠練 習

(1) 每位小朋友到台前來，和老師做以下的問答練習：

老師：She（He）is my student：I like her（him）
and she（he）likes me.

學生：That's right. I'm her（his）student. I like
her（him）and she（he）likes me,

(2) 讓小朋友自行分組，二或三人一組，請他們上來做課文的
對話練習，老師從旁糾正發音。

(3) p.18 的對話練習，可讓小朋友先寫出句子，再2個人一組
上來表演。

♠教學重點

學生們很可能會把 they，we，I，he，she 等和 them，us，
me，him，her 弄混，應耐心練習，讓他們從各種練習中自然
熟練，千萬不可叫小朋友死背。

 習題解答

3-1 LET'S PRACTICE（p.18）

1. A：*Who is that girl*？
   B：*She is Mary's sister. I like her very much.*
   Do you know Mary？

   A：*Yes, I do. I know her. She knows me very*
   well. We are good friends.

2. A：*Who is that woman*？
   B：*She is Mary's mother. I like her very much.*
   Do you know Mary？（以下同第 1 題）

3. A : *Who are they ?*

   B : *They are Helen's brother and sister. I like them very much. Do you know Helen?* (以下同第1題)

4. A : *Who are they ?*

   B : *They are Mary's friends. I like them very much. Do you know Mary ?* (以下同第1題)

3-3 EXERCISE (p.21)

Write and circle.

① I know Mary's sister. But my mother does not know **her** .

② I like my dog. He likes **me** , too.

③ We like Mark. He likes **us** , too.

④ Does your father take **you** to the zoo ?
Yes, he sometimes takes me to the zoo.

⑤ Does Mark have an umbrella with **him** ? No, he does not.

⑥ A: How many hot dogs do you have ?
B: I have four.
A: Are (they, their, them) all for (you, your) ?
A: No. (They, Their, Them) are for John and (I, my, me). They are (we, our, us) lunch. (We, Our, Us) like (they, their, them) very much.

Unit 4

OUR, YOUR AND THEIR

♠ 學習目標

如何使用所有格代名詞如，mine，hers。並複習所有格（your，her...）受格（him，her...）等用法。

♠ 教學方式

(1) 先複習代名詞的所有格，如my，your，his，her，our，their 等等。可利用 p.24 的表格，或讓小朋友自己上來造句。

(2) 告訴小朋友將① This is my book.（這是我的書），改為② This book is my book.（這本書是我的。）時，其中②的 my book 重複，所以要用" mine "取代，變成" This book is mine."

(3) 利用例句介紹 mine，yours，his，hers，ours，theirs 的用法和句型。

♠ 練 習

(1) 先準備好兩種圖片，一種上面畫著曾學過的名詞，如書、雨傘、狗等等，另一種則填上所有格名稱。將學生分為兩組輪流推派一位上前抽這兩種圖片，並利用兩張圖片來造句，如" This is her pen." " This pen is hers."，2 個句子都正確的小朋友方能得分。得分最多那組為優勝隊。

(2) 請每個小朋友交出一樣東西，如課本、鉛筆盒、筆，並在
上面標明自己的英文名字，然後每兩個一組到台前，由老
師指定一件物品來做以下的問答練習。

A : Is this your ～?
B : No, it is not mine.

A : Whose ～ is this?
B : It is＋人名's. The ～ is hers (his).

♠ 教學重點

(1) 代名詞如 I , you , he , she , we , they 等為主格，可做主
詞。其受格為me , you , him , her , us , them , 可做受詞。
其所有代名詞則為mine , yours , his , hers , ours , theirs,
可以等於「所有格＋名詞」，如mine ＝my＋<u>名詞</u> , yours
＝ your ＋<u>名詞</u>… 。

(2) 小朋友可能會將代名詞的受格、主格、所有代名詞混淆，
此時老師要耐心地重覆練習，可利用 p.24 的表格。

(3) 將所有格改為所有代名詞時只要在所有格後面加 s 即可，
但注意mine 和his 例外。

習題解答

4-1 LET'S PRACTICE （p.25）

(1)

2. A : *Whose flower is this?*
   B : *It's Nancy's. The flower is hers.*

3. A : *Whose pencil is this ?*
   B : *It's Mark's. The pencil is his.*

4. A : *Whose picture is this ?*
   B : *It's Wayne's. The picture is his.*

Circle and say.

(2)
1. A: Is this your book ?
   B: Yes, it is (mine, yours).

2. A: This pen is Susan's. Are those
   pens (his, hers), too ?
   B: No, they are not. They are (her
   mother, her mother's).

3. A: How many friends do you have ?
   B: I have two friends. (They, Their,
   Them) names are Mark and
   Nancy.

4-3 EXERCISE (p.27)

Look and write.

(1)

Mary : Good __morning__ , Miss Wang.

Miss Wang : Hi, Mary. You have a beautiful umbrella.

Mary : Oh, it isn't __mine__ .

Miss Wang : Whose umbrella is it?

Mary : It's my __mother's__ .

I am using it today.

(2)

I	my	me	mine
you	your	you	yours
he she it	his her its	him her it	his hers x
Mary	mary's	Mary	Mary's

we	our	us	ours
you	your	you	yours
they	their	them	theirs

Unit 5

IT'S RAINING TODAY

♠ 教學目標

讓小朋友學會如何詢問天氣及晴、雨、陰天的表達方法。

♠ 教學方式

(1)老師先將各種天氣形容詞列在黑板上，由老師帶著小朋友大聲唸。在解釋其中文意思時，儘量用圖片或動作來說明。

(2)介紹「It is ＋天氣形容詞」的句型，此時告訴小朋友 it 是指天氣。

(3)詢問天氣如何時，要用" how "這個疑問詞，而疑問詞要放句首，故「今天天氣如何？」應該說成" How is the weather today？" 程度較好的班級，老師可再教他們「昨天／明天的天氣如何？」的句型。

♠ 練習

(1)課文中的對話部分，包括了前三冊所教過的句型，讓小朋友2個人一組，到台上來表演，再由老師糾正錯誤。

(2)老師準備好數張圖卡，分別表示 warm，hot，cool，cold，sunny，cloudy，rainy，windy，snowy。用點名或輪流的方式請小朋友上來抽三張卡。老師問三個問題：

    1. How's the weather today？

    2. How was the weather yesterday？

3. How will the weather be tomorrow?

小朋友則按照抽到的圖卡來回答。一直到全班都回答過為
止。

(3) 每次上課前,老師可問全班 "How's the weather today?"
增加小朋友練習的機會。

♠ 教學重點

(1) 春、夏、秋、冬四季前用介系詞 in,老師在教這4個單字
時就要加在前面,如「在春天」為 "in spring" 以提醒小
朋友注意。

(2) 在教「昨天/明天的天氣如何?」時,會牽涉到過去式was
及未來式will be 的用法,老師只要讓小朋友像韻律一樣
地唸熟即可,不必解釋太多,避免徒增小朋友學習困擾。

 習題解答

5-1 LET'S PRACTICE (p.30)

1. Spring

A : How's the weather today?

B : It is sunny.

A : How was the weather yesterday?

B : It was cloudy.

A : How will the weather be tomorrow?

B : It will be windy.

2. **Summer**

A : *How's the weather today?*

B : *It is rainy.*

A : *How was the weather yesterday?*

B : *It was rainy.*

A : *How will the weather be tomorrow?*

B : *It will be cloudy.*

3. **Fall**

A : *How's the weather today?*

B : *It is windy*

A : *How was the weather yesterday?*

B : *It was cloudy.*

A : *How will the weather be tomorrow?*

B : *It will be sunny.*

4. **Winter**

A : *How's the weather today?*

B : *It is snowy.*

A : *How was the weather yesterday?*

B : *It is windy.*

A : *How will the weather be tomorrow?*

B : *It will be cloudy.*

5-3 EXERCISE （p.32）

Look and write.

We ski in winter.

We play baseball in spring.

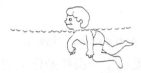

We swim in summer.

We play tennis in fall.

Weather Report

It is rainy today.
I go to school.

It is sunny today.
I wash clothes.

It is cloudy today.
I go shopping.

It is windy today.
I get up early.

It is snowy today.
I read a book.

Unit 6

I CAN RIDE A BICYCLE

♠ 學習目標

學習搭乘各式交通工具的說法：by ＋交通工具，並複習「能夠～」的用法。

♠ 教學方式

(1) 先將本課的生字列在黑板上： ride a bicycle, ride a motorcycle 等等，一邊帶領學生大聲唸，一邊做動作，並讓學生一起做動作。

(2) 再將學過的「主詞＋ can ＋動詞」句型套上新的生詞。等小朋友熟練之後，再讓他們改成否定句及疑問句： I can not ＋動詞，Can you ＋動詞？及 What can you do ？

(3) 講解 " by " 的用法，其中文意思有二個，一為「利用」，一為以前學過的「在～旁邊」，「搭車」則為 " by bus "；可以想成「利用公車」。而「走路」的 " on foot "，可教小朋友想成我們在腳「上面」，由腳帶我們去某地。

♠ 練 習

(1) 將小朋友分為兩組，輪流推選一位到台上，由全體學生問 " How do you go to school ？" 台上的小朋友則用動作表達，並由另一組回答，答對即得分，積分多的一組則獲勝。

(2)請每位小朋友準備一張圖卡，上面畫著他會做的事，如彈鋼琴、騎腳踏車等等，交給老師。上課時，大家圍成圓圈，由老師站在中間，點一個小朋友出來，問他，"What can you do？"，再讓他抽圖卡，並根據抽到的圖卡來回答。答對者，可自行指定另一個小朋友，並問他"What can you do？"，再讓他抽圖卡來回答。若答錯，則出局。由老師再點一個小朋友出來，從新開始。一直到每位小朋友都答過為止。最後，答錯的小朋友可罰他們唱歌。

♠ **教學重點**

(1)向小朋友大概說明 can 為助動詞，所以第三人稱單數時不必加 s。

(2)「by＋交通工具」時，不必在交通工具前加任何冠詞 a 或 the，注意糾正學生的錯誤。

(3)本課出現一些新的動詞，如 ride，fly，drive，dance 等，向小朋友說明當這些動詞第三人稱單數加 s 時的語尾變化和發音。

(4)"can not"可以縮寫成"can't"，注意小朋友 can't 的發音和 can 的差別。

習題解答

6-1 LET'S PRACTICE（p.35）

1. A：*Can you dance*？

   B：*Yes, I can.*

A : *Can you play the piano, too?*

B : *No, I can't. But my mother can play the piano very well.*

2. A : *Can you speak English?*

B : *Yes, I can.*

A : *Can you play baseball, too?*

B : *No, I can't. But my father can play baseball very well.*

3. A : *Can you ride a bicycle?*

B : *Yes, I can.*

A : *Can you ride a horse, too?*

B : *No, I can't. But my father can ride a horse very well.*

4. A : *Can you ride a motorcycle?*

B : *Yes, I can.*

A : *Can you fly an airplane, too?*

B : *No, I can't. But my father can fly an airplane very well.*

5. A : *Can you drive a car?*

B : *Yes, I can.*

A : *Can you ride a horse, too?*

B : *No, I can't. But my father can ride a horse very well.*

6. A : *Can you play basketball ?*
   B : *Yes, I can.*

   A : *Can you play the violin, too ?*
   B : *No, I can't. But my father can play the violin very well.*

6-3 EXERCISE （p.37）

Write and say.

My name is _____*Mary*_____ .
I am___*ten*___ years old.
I live in _____*Taipei*_____ .
I get up at ___*eight*___ o'clock.
I go to school by _____*bus*_____ .
And I can ___*play the piano*___ .
What can you do ?

Unit 7

I AM OLDER THAN YOU

♠ 學習目標

練習比較級與最高級的句型。

♠ 教學方式

(1)將本課生字列在黑板上,帶小朋友大聲唸,並儘量用動作來解釋意思,千萬不要讓小朋友死背單字。

(2)講解什麼是「比較級」和「最高級」,並將黑板上的形容詞生字改為比較級和最高級,並讓小朋友上來改。改完後,讓小朋友跟讀,一直到他們能朗朗上口為止。

(3)告訴小朋友如何造一個比較級的句子。首先將一個形容詞找出來加 er,再找出 2 個要比較的東西,如:「我比你年輕。」,英文應該是 " I am younger than you." 其中 " than " 是「比」的意思,而且一定要放在形容詞後面;告訴小朋友這是英文的規定,就像第三人稱單數動詞要加 s 一樣。

(4)介紹「as + 形容詞 as 」的用法,先讓小朋友利用以前學過的形容詞,到黑板上來寫如 as big as 、as old as 、as tall as 等詞語,等他們唸熟了之後再加上前後 2 個名詞和 be 動詞。

(5)當小朋友發現有些形容詞的比較級和最高級不是加 er 和 est 時，告訴他們因為這些字太長了，加 er 或 est 不好唸，所以要加 more 和 most 。

(6)說明最高級的句型時，先教小朋友如「最高的男孩」、「最矮的女孩」該怎麼說，待他們自己會說這些詞語之後，再加上完整的句子。如 the tallest boy → He is the tallest boy. → He is the tallest boy in our class.

♠ 練　習

(1)讓小朋友 4 個人一組；玩接龍造句遊戲，每一個小朋友想一個東西，第二個小朋友想一個形容詞，第三個小朋友想另一個可與第一個東西比較的名詞，第 4 個小朋友，就利用這些名詞和形容詞造一個比較級的句子。每位小朋友在說完之後就蹲下，第 4 位小朋友造完句後，就走到第一個小朋友的位置蹲下，其他三位依次後退，再重新造句。老師可隨時喊停，請一組小朋友出來表演。

(2)老師可準備數組圖卡，或利用本課的插圖，讓小朋友 2 個人一組，上來抽一組圖卡 3 張，利用這 3 張圖卡，造一個比較級和最高級的句子，答對者可回座，答錯者要跟著老師大聲唸三次。

(3)指定學生回家紀錄全家人的身高、體重、年齡等，下次上課可請他們報告家中誰最高、最胖、最小等。

♠ 教學重點

(1)提醒小朋友最高級之前一定要加 the 。

(2)給小朋友比較級句型公式：<u>主詞 1</u>＋ be 動詞＋<u>形容詞</u>＋
er ＋ than ＋<u>主詞 2</u>

(3)可利用小朋友以前學過的形容詞作更多的練習，並提醒他
們字較長的形容詞的比較級和最高級需要用 more 和 most。

習題解答

7-1 LET'S PRACTICE （p.39, 40）

（P39）1. *Helen is taller than Nancy.*
Nancy is shorter than Helen.

2. *The elephant is bigger than the mouse.*
The mouse is smaller than the elephant.

3. *Father is older than John.*
John is younger than Father.

4. *The train is faster than the bike.*
The bike is slower than the train.

5. *The city is noisier than the country.*
The country is quieter than the city.

6. *The ballpoint pen is cheaper than the pen.*
The pen is more expensive than the ballpoint pen.

（P40）1. A: *Helen's doll is better than Mary's.*
B: *Susan's doll is better than Helen's.*
A: *Susan's doll is the best of the three dolls.*

2. A : *Susan's skirt is longer than Mary's.*
   B : *Helen's skirt is longer than Susan's.*
   A : *Helen's skirt is the longest of the three skirts.*

3. A : *The elephant is bigger than the lion.*
   B : *The lion is bigger than the cat.*
   A : *The elephant is the biggest of the three animals.*

4. A : *Nancy's dress is more beautiful than Helen's.*
   B : *Susan's dress is more beautiful than Nancy's.*
   A : *Susan's dress is the most beautiful of the three girls'.*

7-3 EXERCISE (p. 42)

Look and say.

1. Who is taller, John or Mary ?
   John is <u>*taller*</u> <u>*than*</u> <u>*Mary*</u> .

2. The elephant is <u>*stronger*</u> <u>*than*</u> the giraffe.
   The giraffe is <u>*stronger*</u> <u>*than*</u> the dog.
   The elephant is the <u>*strongest*</u> of the three.

3. A is bigger <u>*than*</u> B.
   C is <u>*smaller*</u> than B.
   C is <u>*the*</u> <u>*smallest*</u> box.

4. The bicycle is <u>*cheaper*</u> <u>*than*</u> the motorcycle.
   The motorcycle is <u>*cheaper*</u> <u>*than*</u> the car.
   The car is <u>*the*</u> <u>*most expensive*</u> of the three.

Unit 8

I WAS IN TAIPEI LAST YEAR

♠ 教學目標

學習過去式的句型，教小朋友將現在式動詞改過去式動詞。

♠ 教學方式

(1) 先跟小朋友解釋「現在式」是指發生在「現在」，或是「固定會發生」的事情，如「每天上學、起床」等。而「過去式」則是指發生在過去的事情。如「昨天看了一場電影」；「昨天晚上看電視」等等。在英文裡頭，是由「動詞」來判定時態的，所以將一個現在式的句子改爲過去式的句子，只要把動詞改一下即可。

(2) 先在黑板上寫出幾個以前學過的動詞，如 is，are，cook，wash，play 等等，再請小朋友上來用這些動詞造句。之後再帶他們複習跟讀這些現在式的例句。

(3) 教小朋友將黑板上的例句，改爲過去式。先請他們注意動詞部分的更改原則；$\begin{matrix} is \\ are \end{matrix}$ 改爲 $\begin{matrix} was \\ were \end{matrix}$，其它動詞則在字尾加 ed，然後再加上一個表示過去的時間，如 yesterday、last night 等。解釋完之後，請小朋友上來改黑板上的句子。

(4) 用例句告訴小朋友過去式的否定句，只要將原來現在式中的 " don't 或 doesn't " 改爲 " didn't " 即可。而過去式的疑問句也只要把 " do 或 does " 改爲 " did " 即可。

(5) was 和 were 因爲是從 is 和 are 變成的，所以它們的否定句和疑問句就和 is、are 一樣。否定句直接在後面加 not，疑問句則把 was 和 were 搬到句首。同樣請小朋友上來改寫句子。

(6) 帶讀黑板上的句子，直到他們熟練爲止。

♠練 習

(1) 小朋友分成 2 組，每組輪流派一個小朋友上台來造一個現在式的句子；將句子寫在黑板上並大聲唸一遍，由另一組的小朋友一起來改成過去式的句子。回答正確又整齊劃一者得 2 分，回答零零落落者，只得一分。一直玩到每位小朋友都上來造過句爲止，得分高的那組獲勝，老師可給一些獎賞，激發他們的榮譽心。

(2) 首先由老師點班長出來，問："What did you do yester-day？"，班長要用過去式來回答，若回答正確，則由他指定另一個小朋友，問他同樣的問題，老師可在旁指導。答錯的小朋友不可指定他人來問問題，所以由老師來指定。注意不可重覆指定同一個小朋友，直到全班都玩過爲止。

(3) 等小朋友熟練(2)的練習後，可將問句的句型改爲"What did he（she、they …）do last night（year、month …）？"等等，繼續玩。

♠重 點

(1) 過去式的動詞分爲「規則變化」和「不規則變化」2 種，本課先介紹「規則變化」，即字尾加 ed 的變化。

(2) 注意 ed 的唸法；在有聲子音之後唸 / d / ，在無聲子音之後唸 / t / 。此外，可向小朋友解釋本課中的 visited ，shouted ，painted 等字，若照規定 ed 應唸成 / t / ，但是 2 個 / t / 遇到一起，不好發音，故都應唸成 / tɪd / 。

(3) 同樣地，字尾爲 d 的動詞，加 ed 時也應唸爲 / d / ，但 2 個 / d / 不好唸，所以也要唸成 / dɪd / 。

(4) 在向小朋友說明過去式時，儘量用以前學過的單字，等他們較熟悉之後，再教生字，以免小朋友負荷過重。

(5) 老師可根據小朋友的程度，將本課分成數次教完。

 習題解答

8-1　LET'S PRACTICE　（p.46）

I : 1. *What did you do yesterday?*
　　　I painted a picture.

　　2. *What did you do last Saturday?*
　　　I played tennis with my friends.

　　3. *What did you do last night?*
　　　I cooked dinner.

　　4. *What did you do yesterday morning?*
　　　I walked to school.

II : 1. *Did you watch TV yesterday?*
　　　No, I didn't. I didn't watch TV yesterday.

2. *Did you play baseball yesterday?*
   No, I didn't. I didn't play baseball yesterday.

3. *Did you talk to John yesterday?*
   No, I didn't. I didn't talk to John yesterday.

4. *Did you visit Mark yesterday?*
   No, I didn't. I didn't visit Mark yesterday.

5. *Did you listen to records yesterday?*
   No, I didn't. I didn't listen to records yesterday.

6. *Did you stay at home yesterday.*
   No, I didn't. I didn't stay at home yesterday.

8-3 EXERCISE (p.48)

(1) Fill in the blanks (was or were).
   was, was, was, was, were, were

(2) Make sentences.

   ② We invited them for dinner last night.

   ③ Mark washed dishes last night.

   ④ Mary was in Taipei last year.

   ⑤ She cleaned the living room last Sunday.

   ⑥ They listened to records last night.

Unit 9

A HOLIDAY

♠教學目標

練習不規則動詞變化的過去式。

♠教學方式

(1)向小朋友介紹另一種動詞過去式的改法；但千萬不要他們死背這些不規則變化，而是由不斷的帶讀來讓他們朗朗上口。

(2)將本課提及的不規則變化動詞以詞組的方式寫在黑板上，

如 $\begin{cases} \text{get up early} \\ \text{got up early} \end{cases}$ ，$\begin{cases} \text{go to school} \\ \text{went to school} \end{cases}$ 等，讓小朋友大聲朗頌，直到像韻律般地脫口而出為止。

(3)再將詞組套入肯定句、否定句、疑問句中帶讀，並介紹一些新的表過去時間的說法。

(4)老師可視學生的接受程度，將本課的不規則變化分次上完。在每次上課開始，可幫學生複習上次教過的動詞變化。

♠練 習

(1)與第8課相同的練習活動，此時，老師可指定一些不規則變化的動詞，寫在黑板上，讓學生造句。

♠ **教學重點**

(1) 老師每次上課時，都可以幫小朋友複習不規則動詞的過去式；初學的小朋友，可能會被攪混，老師一定要有耐心，用反覆練習，讓他們熟記。

(2) 接受力強的學生，可為其說明字尾為 y 的動詞，加 ed 過去式時的變化：子音＋y →去 y＋ied；母音＋y → yed（如 stu<u>dy</u> → stud<u>ied</u>；pl<u>ay</u> → play<u>ed</u>）

 習題解答

9-1 LET'S PRACTICE（p.52）

1. A : *Did Mary sleep well last night?*
   B : *Yes, she did. She was very tired.*

   A : *Why? What did she do yesterday?*
   B : *She worked hard.*

2. A : *Did John sleep well last night?*
   B : *Yes, he did. He was very tired.*

   A : *Why? What did he do yesterday?*
   B : *He cleaned his room.*

3. A : *Did Tom sleep well last night?*
   B : *Yes, he did. He was very tired.*

   A : *Why? What did he do yesterday?*
   B : *He washed the windows.*

4. A : *Did Peter sleep well last night ?*
   B : *Yes, he did. He was very tired.*

   A : *Why ? What did he do yesterday ?*
   B : *He studied English.*

5. A : *Did Susan sleep well last night ?*
   B : *Yes, she did. She was very tired.*

   A : *Why ? What did she do yesterday ?*
   B : *She wrote letters.*

9-3 EXERCISE （p.54）

A: Did you go to school by car the day before yesterday ?
B: No, ___I___ didn't .
A: How ___did___ ___you___ ___go___ to school ?
B: I went to school by bicycle.

A: Did you come home at 5:00 yesterday ?
B: No, I didn't .
A: When did you come home ?
B: I came home at 5:15 yesterday.

A: Did you sing a song last night ?
B: No, I didn't .
A: What did you do ?
B: I wrote a letter.

A: Did you eat your breakfast yesterday ?
B: Yes, I did.
A: What did you eat ?
B: I had bread and milk.

A: Did you see a tiger in the zoo ?
B: No, I didn't .
A: What did you see ?
B: I saw a giraffe.

Unit　10

I WAS RUNNING

♠ 教學目標

過去進行式的使用 。

♠ 教學方法

(1) 先幫小朋友複習以前學過的「現在進行式」；直到他們可以自己造句爲止 。

(2) 舉例解釋「現在進行式」和「過去進行式」，如「現在正在看電視」用現在進行式 " is watching TV"，若要表示「昨天正在看電視」，就要用「過去進行式」。

(3)「過去進行式」的改法，只要把 is 改成 was ，are 改成 were 即可 。

(4) 請小朋友將自己造的「現在進行式」句子，改爲「過去進行式」，並大聲帶讀 。

(5) 用口頭練習的方式 ，將「過去進行式」的肯定句改爲否定句及疑問句 。

(6) 用問答練習的方式說明第 56 頁 while 的句型，並解釋中文意思 。

♠ 練　習

(1) 老師準備圖卡數張 ，上面畫著各種動作（ 或利用 p.57 的插圖 ），蓋住放在台前 。輪流或點名請小朋友到台前來 ，讓小朋友抽圖卡，並根據圖卡來造「現在進行式」的句子。圖卡也可由小朋友來製做，下面幾課還會用到。

(2) 每個小朋友準備一張同(1)的圖卡，拿到胸前，圍成一個圓圈。老師先找志願者出來，問他 "What were you doing?"，讓他根據自己的圖卡來回答。然後，老師可指著Mary（任何一個班上同學）問："What was Mary doing？"讓他看著Mary 的圖卡來回答。都答對了之後，再由志願者點一個小朋友出來，像老師一樣，問他上述2個問題。不會回答的同學，由老師從旁指導。

(3) 在使用圖卡時，先讓每個小朋友上台來，用中文和英文解釋圖卡上的動作。

♠ 教學重點

(1) 老師在剛開始教新單字時，不必要求學生背下來。只要小朋友能看圖唸出正確的拼音即可，因此可多利用口頭練習。待他們熟練之後，再開始書寫的練習。

(2) 「過去進行式」句型公式：was／were + Ving

10-1 LET'S PRACTICE （p.57）

1. A : *Were you studying English yesterday evening*?
   B : *Yes, I was.*

2. A : *Were you studying English yesterday evening?*
   B : *No, I wasn't.*

   A : *What were you doing?*
   B : *I was watching TV.*

3. A : *Were you studying English yesterday evening?*
   B : *No, I wasn't.*

   A : *What were you doing?*
   B : *I was dancing with my friends.*

4. A : *Were you studying English yesterday evening?*
   B : *No, I wasn't.*

   A : *What were you doing?*
   B : *I was playing basketball.*

5. A : *Were you studying English yesterday evening?*
   B : *No, I wasn't.*

   A : *What were you doing?*
   B : *I was preparing dinner.*

6. A : *Were you studying English yesterday evening?*
   B : *No, I wasn't.*

   A : *What were you doing?*
   B : *I was writing a letter.*

10-3 EXERCISE （p.59）

Look and write.

1. Susan met Mary while she was shopping.

2. Tom lost his wallet while he was washing his hands.

3. John got hurt while he was playing baseball.

4. Nancy met Helen while she was waiting for the bus.

5. Mother cut herself while she was preparing dinner.

Unit 11

WHAT ARE YOU LOOKING FORWARD TO?

♠ **教學目標**

未來式 be going to 的句型。

♠ **教學方式**

(1) 告訴小朋友以前已學過「現在式」和、「過去式」，今天要開始學「未來式」。例如：「明天將要去看電影」這句話在英文裡就是「未來式」。

(2) 「未來式」也是在句子的「動詞」做變化，這次有 2 種變化，都可以改成「未來式」，即加 " will " 或 " be going to "，它們都是「將要」的意思。

(3) 先在黑板上列出：

I am going to	He is going to
You are going to	She is going to
They are going to	We are going to

並帶小朋友跟讀，讓他們朗朗上口。待他們唸熟之後，老師可唸 <u>I</u> ，讓小朋友一起接唸 <u>am going to</u> ，如此反覆練習。

(4) 將黑板上的例句加上以前學過的動詞，和表未來式的時間，如 tomorrow，next week 等。用動作向小朋友解釋句意，並請小朋友一邊跟著唸，一邊做動作。

(5) 用(3)的方式，帶小朋友唸否定句及疑問句。

♠ 練 習

(1)請小朋友回家用「未來式」be going to 的句型寫下明天
將做哪些事，下次上課上台來報告給全班同學聽。

(2)老師準備好 5 張卡片，上面分別寫上 you，he，she，they，
we，拿在手上，不讓小朋友看到。請小朋友自行分組，2
個人一組，一個當 A，一個當 B，拿著自己製作的圖卡（上
一課用過的即可）到台前來，由老師抽一張卡片當做主詞，
讓他們根據自己的圖卡做以下的問答：

A：Be 動詞＋老師抽的主詞 going to A 的圖卡 tomorrow?

B：No，主詞＋Be 動詞 not.

A：What＋Be 動詞 主詞 going to do?

B：主詞＋Be 動詞 going to B 的圖卡.

♠ 教學重點

(1)本課的練習以 " be going to " 的句型爲主；" will " 的句
型爲下一課的重點。

(2)適度的背誦有助於小朋友以英文思考及糾正發音錯誤；因
此可讓他們背誦課文，於課堂上背誦；表現優異者可給予
獎品。

習題解答

11-1 LET'S PRACTICE （p.61）

1. John : *Are you going to school tomorrow?*

   Tom : *No, I'm not. I went to school yesterday.*

   John : *What are you going to do?*

   Tom : *I'm going to swim.*

2. Tom : *Are you going to play the piano tonight?*
   Susan: *No, I'm not . I played the piano yesterday.*

   Tom : *What are you going to do?*
   Susan: *I'm going to see a movie.*

3. Tom: *Are you going to play football tomorrow night ?*
   John & Paul : *No, we aren't. We played football yesterday.*

   Tom: *What are you going to do?*
   John & Paul : *We are going to dance.*

4. Tom: *Are you going to ride a bicycle next week ?*
   Peter & Jack: *No, we aren't. We rode a bicycle yesterday.*

   Tom: *What are you going to do ?*
   Peter & Jack: *We are going to drive a car.*

5. Tom : *Are you going to swim tomorrow afternoon?*
   Mary : *No, I'm not . I swam last week.*

   Tom : *What are you going to do ?*
   Mary : *I'm going to ski.*

6. Tom: *Are you going to eat ice cream tonight ?*
   Mark & Nancy: *No, we aren't. We ate ice cream this morning.*

Tom: *What are you going to eat?*

Mark & Nancy: *We are going to eat hamburgers.*

11-3 EXERCISE (p.63)

①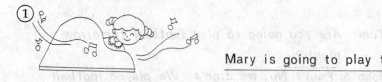

Mary is going to play the piano.

②

Susan is looking forward to
playing tennis.

③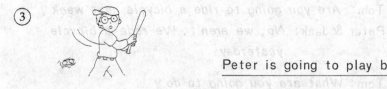

Peter is going to play baseball.

④

John is going to buy a radio.

⑤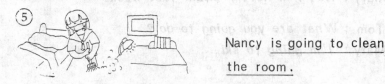

Nancy is going to clean
the room.

⑥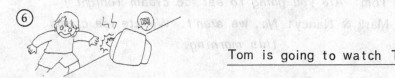

Tom is going to watch TV.

Unit 12

JOHN'S TIMETABLE FOR TOMORROW

♠ **教學目標**

未來式「 will ＋原形動詞」的句型應用 。

♠ **教學方式：**

(1) 複習上一課未來式 " be going to " 的句型，由老師問學生 " What are you going to do tomorrow？ " ，將學生的回答寫在黑板上 ，並在每句的 " be going to " 部分劃線 ，或用有顏色的粉筆書寫 。

(2) 介紹 " will " 這個字也是「 將要 」之意 ，因此可以代替句子中的 " be going to " 的部分。請小朋友上來改寫句子 ，並帶讀 。

(3) 告訴小朋友 " will " 是屬於「 助動詞 」，像 " can " 一樣 ，否定句直接加 not ，疑問句則搬到句首 。

(4) 在教本課的單字時 ，可和小朋友玩「 比手劃腳 」的遊戲 ，老師每教一個生字 ，就請一位小朋友上來 ，由老師偷偷將中文意思告訴他 ，讓他比手劃腳 ，但不能出聲 ，請其它小朋友來猜 。

♠ **練 習**

(1) 輪流請小朋友出來由老師唸一個現在式的句子 ，請小朋友改為「 未來式 will 」的句型 。

(2)每位小朋友將自製的動作圖卡拿到胸前，2個人一組到台
前來，做以下的問答練習：

   A：What will you do tomorrow？

   B：I will <u>B的圖卡</u> tomorrow. What will you do
tomorrow？

   A：I will <u>A的圖卡</u> tomorrow.

(3)請每位小朋友將自己明天的活動寫成如 P.64 的表格，拿
到胸前，圍成圓圈。老師站在中間，每次點2名小朋友A、
B出來，根據他們的功課表和A、B做問答，老師問A：
"Will B study Chinese at four o'clock tomorrow
evening？"圖卡A則根據B的圖卡回答 yes 或 no 的句子。
然後老師再讓B看著A的圖卡問B問題。

(4)請小朋友回家利用自己寫的表格，準備一份小報告，下次
上課由老師抽點同學上來用未來式報告明天的活動。

♠ **教學重點**

(1) will not 可縮寫成 won't。

(2)本課可連帶為小朋友複習時間的說法。

習題解答

12-1 LET'S PRACTICE （p.66）

1. A：*Will Nancy go swimming this evening？*

  B：*Yes, she will. She will go swimming.*

2. A：*Will Tom, Peter, and Susan play frisbee tomorrow?*

  B：*Yes, they will. They will play frisbee tomorrow.*

3. A : *Will Mary and John go shopping tomorrow?*
   B : *Yes, they will. They will go shopping tomorrow.*

4. A : *Will you visit a friend in the hospital tomorrow?*
   B : *Yes, I will. I will visit a friend in the hospital.*

5. A : *Will your father read newspapers tonight?*
   B : *Yes, he will. He will read newspapers tonight.*

6. A : *Will Helen clean her room tomorrow?*
   B : *Yes, she will. She will clean her room.*

12-3 EXERCISE （p.68）

Read and write.

A : Where <u>will</u> <u>you</u> <u>be</u> tonight?
B : They <u>will</u> <u>be</u> at home.
A : What <u>will</u> <u>they</u> <u>do</u> there?
B : They <u>will</u> study English.

A : Where <u>will</u> <u>he</u> <u>be</u> tomorrow?
B : <u>He</u> <u>will</u> <u>be</u> <u>at</u> home.
A : What <u>will</u> <u>he</u> <u>do</u> there?
B : He <u>will</u> <u>wash</u> the kitchen floor.

A : <u>Where</u> <u>will</u> <u>she</u> <u>be</u> this evening?
B : <u>She</u> <u>will</u> <u>be</u> in the kitchen.
A : <u>What</u> <u>will</u> <u>she</u> <u>do</u> there?
B : <u>She</u> <u>will</u> bake cookies.

第 四 冊 學 習 內 容 一 覽 表

單元	內　　　容	練　　　習	活　　　動	習　　作
複習第三冊	(1) 他們在哪裏？ (2) 現在進行式？ (3) 簡單式 (4) 早餐、午餐和晚餐 (5) 日常生活	Look and read. Look and say. Look and say. Look and say. Sing a song.		
1	我的學校	Look and say：看圖練習 How many～？與 first, second 等序數的問答。	遊戲：A road game	Read and write.
2	生日快樂	Look and read：看月曆學習日期的說法。	遊戲：When is your birthday？	Look and write.
3	他和她	Look and say：看插圖練習受格 him, her, me 等的用法。	遊戲：Learn a rhyme	Write and circle.
4	我們的，你們的和他們的	Look and say：從例圖中練習名詞所有格 mine, yours, hers 的用法。	遊戲：Make a guess	Look and write.
5	今天是下雨天	Look and say：看圖練習 How's the weather today？的問與答。	歌曲：You are my sunshine	Look and write.
6	你如何去學校？	Look and say：看插圖練習 can 的句型代換。	勞作：Make a boat	Write and say.
7	我比你大	Look and say：從給予的圖片中練習比較級和最高級的句型。	遊戲：Make a guess	Look and write
8	我去年在台北	Look and say：看圖練習過去式的句型問答。（規則動詞變化）	歌曲：Old MacDonald had a farm	① Fill in the blanks. ② Make sentences.
9	放假日	Read and practice：練習過去式的不規則動詞變化，看圖代換問答。	歌曲：Twinkle twinkle little star	Look and write.
10	我正在跑步	Look and say：看例圖練習過去進行式的句型問答。	遊戲：Body quiz	Look and write.
11	你正期待著什麼？	Look and say：看例圖練習未來式 be going to 的問與答。	歌曲：The sun is shining	Read and write.
12	約翰明天的功課表	Look and say：看圖練習未來式 will 的問與答。	遊戲：Find your way	Read and write.
複習	(1) 遊戲 (2) 口頭練習 (3) 生字總復習	A crossword puzzle Ask and answer Picture dictionary		

LEARNING
English Readers for Children 5

Let's Start with English

習題解答 | Review 2 Who is the fattest?

Look and say. （p.4）

2. A : *How many animals are there in the picture?*
   B : *There are four animals in the picture.*

   A : *Which is the strongest?*
   B : *The monkey is the strongest.*

   A : *Which is the thinnest?*
   B : *The rat is the thinnest.*

   A : *Is the rat taller than the giraffe?*
   B : *No, the rat is shorter than the giraffe.*

   A : *Do you know who is the shortest?*
   B : *The rat is the shortest.*

3. A : *How many dogs are there in the picture?*
   B : *There are four dogs in the picture.*

   A : *Which is the oldest?*
   B : *The yellow one is the oldest.*

   A : *Which is the youngest?*
   B : *The brown one is the youngest.*

   A : *Is the blue one taller than the yellow one?*
   B : *No, the blue one is shorter than the yellow one.*

A : *Do you know which is the shortest* ?

B : *The blue one is the shortest .*

4. A : *How many people are there in the picture* ?

B : *There are four people in the picture .*

A : *Who is the fattest* ?

B : *The last one is the fattest .*

A : *Who is the thinnest* ?

B : *The third one is the thinnest .*

A : *Is the last one taller than the third one* ?

B : *No, the last one is shorter than the third one.*

A : *Do you know who is the shortest* ?

B : *The last one is the shortest .*

Review 4 〉 **I will study English** (p.6)

Look and say.

2. A : *What will you do after dinner this evening* ?

B : *I will play volleyball .*

A : *Will you play volleyball tomorrow* ?

B : *Yes, I will. (No, I will not.)*

3. A : *What will you do after dinner this evening* ?

B : *I will go to the movies .*

A : *Will you go to the movies tomorrow* ?

B : *Yes, I will. (No, I will not.)*

4. A : *What will you do after dinner this evening?*
   B : *I will clean the floor.*

   A : *Will you clean the floor tomorrow?*
   B : *Yes, I will. (No, I will not.)*

                    *   *   *

2. A : *Are you going to take a walk tomorrow?*
   B : *Yes, I am going to take a walk tomorrow.*

   A : *Who is going to be with you?*
   B : *My friend is going to be with me.*

3. A : *Are you going to swim tomorrow?*
   B : *Yes, I am going to swim tomorrow.*

   A : *Who is going to be with you?*
   B : *My friend is going to be with me.*

4. A : *Are you going to ski tomorrow?*
   B : *Yes, I am going to ski tomorrow.*

   A : *Who is going to be with you?*
   B : *My friend is going to be with me.*

UNIT 1

MARY IS A GOOD GIRL

♠ 學習目標

讓小朋友能夠正確地使用頻率副詞如：always, usually, often, sometimes 及 never。

♠ 教學方式

(1) 先利用圖片向小朋友介紹除了頻率副詞以外的生字，如 bread, sandwich, hamburger 等，待小朋友將這些生字記熟之後，再帶入句子中，注意先不要加上頻率副詞。如：In the morning I eat bread. On Sunday we go to the beach. 至他們能自行造句為止。

(2) 然後告訴小朋友：「當有人問你，多久吃一次漢堡，多久看一次電影時怎樣辦呢？」接下來就可介紹頻率副詞出場了。

(3) 先將 always, usually, often, sometimes 及 never 寫在黑板上，告訴小朋友它們各別的意義（此時可利用 p.9 的百分比表）。再將它們帶入句子當中，放在主詞和動詞之間。由老師帶讀，小朋友一邊作動作，一邊跟讀。

♠ 練 習

(1) 先準備好數張卡片，寫上 100％，85％，65％，35％ 及 0％，讓每個小朋友各抽一張。告訴他們這些數字所代表的意義（參閱 p.9 之表）。當老師說 " always " 時，拿到

100％卡片的小朋友（們）就要站起來，輪流用 always 造
一個句子，老師再將這些小朋友造的句子寫在黑板上，詢
問全班的意見，再指正錯誤，直到每個小朋友都練習過爲
止。

(2)每位小朋友自行準備好一張畫著動作的圖卡，如看電視、
打排球、上英語課等，然後在圖卡背面寫下任何一個頻率
副詞。老師在做活動前，可將每位小朋友的圖卡動作用英
文複習一遍，然後每次點 2 名小朋友出來，輪流根據 2 人
的圖卡作如下的對話。

① A： Do you ever ＋ <u>B 圖卡上的動作</u>？
　 B： Yes. I ＋ <u>B 圖卡背面的頻率副詞</u>＋<u>B 圖卡上的動作</u>。

② B： Do you ever ＋ <u>A 圖卡上的動作</u>？
　 A： Yes. I ＋<u>A 圖卡背面的頻率副詞</u>＋<u>A 圖卡的動作</u>。

♠ **教學重點**

(1)此課有許多新加的生字，再加上頻率副詞的用法，內容頗
多，老師宜分配好上課時數。

(2)強調頻率副詞所放的位置：

① 名詞＋頻率副詞＋動詞＋受詞
② 名詞＋ be 動詞＋頻率副詞＋形容詞

習題解答　**1-1　LET'S PRACTICE**（p.9）

Look and say.

1. ① A : *Do you ever watch TV on Monday*?
   　　B : *No, I don't.*
   　　A : *When do you watch TV*?
   　　B : *I always watch TV on Sunday.*

   ② A : *Do you ever watch TV on Monday*?
   　　B : *No, I don't.*
   　　A : *When do you watch TV*?
   　　B : *I usually watch TV on Sunday.*

   ③ A : *Do you ever watch TV on Monday*?
   　　B : *No, I don't.*
   　　A : *When do you watch TV*?
   　　B : *I often watch TV on Sunday.*

2. ① A : *Do you ever take a bus on Sunday*?
   　　B : *No, I don't.*
   　　A : *When do you take a bus*?
   　　B : *I always take a bus on Monday.*

   ② A : *Do you ever take a bus on Sunday*?
   　　B : *No, I don't.*
   　　A : *When do you take a bus*?
   　　B : *I often take a bus on Monday.*

③ A : *Do you ever take a bus on Sunday ?*
B : *No, I don't.*
A : *When do you take a bus ?*
B : *I sometimes take a bus on Monday.*

3. ① A : *Do you ever clean the living room on Monday ?*
B : *No, I don't.*
A : *When do you clean the living room ?*
B : *I usually clean the living room on Sunday.*

② A : *Do you ever clean the living room on Monday ?*
B : *No, I don't.*
A : *When do you clean the living room ?*
B : *I often clean the living room on Sunday.*

③ A : *Do you ever clean the living room on Monday ?*
B : *No, I don't.*
A : *When do you clean the living room ?*
B : *I never clean the living room.*

4. ① A : *Do you ever go to English class on Sunday ?*
B : *No, I don't.*
A : *When do you go to English class ?*
B : *I always go to English class on Monday.*

② A : *Do you ever go to English class on Sunday ?*
B : *No, I don't.*
A : *When do you go to English class ?*
B : *I sometimes go to English class on Monday.*

③ A : *Do you ever go to English class on Sunday ?*
　 B : *No, I don't.*
　 A : *When do you go to English class ?*
　 B : *I never go to English class.*

5. ① A : *Do you ever drink milk in the evening ?*
　　 B : *No, I don't.*
　　 A : *When do you drink milk ?*
　　 B : *I usually drink milk in the morning.*

　 ② A : *Do you ever drink milk in the evening ?*
　　 B : *No, I don't.*
　　 A : *When do you drink milk ?*
　　 B : *I sometimes drink milk in the morning.*

　 ③ A : *Do you ever drink milk in the evening ?*
　　 B : *No, I don't.*
　　 A : *When do you drink milk ?*
　　 B : *I never drink milk.*

6. ① A : *Do you ever brush your teeth at noon ?*
　　 B : *No, I don't.*
　　 A : *When do you brush your teeth ?*
　　 B : *I often brush my teeth in the morning.*

　 ② A : *Do you ever brush your teeth at noon ?*
　　 B : *No, I don't.*
　　 A : *When do you brush your teeth ?*
　　 B : *I sometimes brush my teeth in the morning.*

③ A : *Do you ever brush your teeth at noon?*
B : *No, I don't.*
A : *When do you brush your teeth?*
B : *I never brush my teeth after the meal.*

1-3 EXERCISE (p.11)

Rearrange the sentences.

1. *Do you always watch television in the evening?*

2. *I never go to school late.*

3. *She usually goes to work by train.*

4. *Are you often busy on Sunday?*

5. *John and Mary always walk to school.*

6. *Jack usually plays in the park.*

UNIT 2

QUANTITY (I)

♠ 學習目標

讓小朋友學會如何使用數量詞 some, any, a few, a little 等，及了解它們所代表數量的多寡。

♠ 教學方式

(1) 老師在教 some 這個字時，可利用圖片教學生唸 some toys, some stamps, some pencils 等詞語，並讓學生看圖了解 some 的意思。之後再將 some 代進句子中。以下 no, a few, a little 亦同。

(2) 先將課文中的可數名詞和不可數名詞，向小朋友解釋清楚。如：water, milk, money 都不能一個一個地數，所以它們是不可數名詞。小朋友可能對於 money 是不可數名詞不太能理解，此時應告訴他們，錢有很多種形態：硬幣、紙鈔等都是，故為不可數。

(3) 教小朋友區別 some（一些）和 a few（少數幾個）在意義上的不同。此外 some 可加不可數名詞，如 some money，但 a few 不可加；a little（少許）才能加不可數名詞。

(4) 告訴學生會用 some, a few, a little 之後，有時候要問別人 " 有沒有 " 時怎麼辦呢？這時候就要用 any（任何）來問了。改疑問句時，將主詞、動詞搬個家，再將 some, a few 等換成 any 即可。

♠ 練 習

老師先準備許多圖片，畫上各種可數及不可數名詞的圖案，將
小朋友分成兩組，輪流出來抽卡片。老師再問抽卡的小朋友：
Is / Are there any～？小朋友則回答：Yes, there is / are
some～.、There is a little～. 或 There are a few～. 若老
師所問的名詞不是卡片裏的圖時，小朋友就須用否定句回答。
完全答對才能得分。分數較多者為優勝隊。

♠ 教學重點

(1) some 多用在肯定句，any 用在疑問句，應讓小朋友反覆練
習，朗朗上口為止。

(2) some + { 可數名詞   any + { 可數名詞
             不可數名詞   不可數名詞

　　a few + 可數名詞
　　a little + 不可數名詞

2-1 LET'S PRACTICE （p.14）

Read and match.

There are some broken chairs in the classroom.

There is only a little food in the refrigerator.

I'm sorry! I don't have any money to pay you.

There isn't any milk in the bottle.

They found a few toys under the bed.

2-3 EXERCISE （p.16）

Answer questions.

1. Does Susan have any toys?
   Yes, she has some toys.

2. How many toys do you have?
   I have many toys.

3. Who has some stamps?
   Peter has some stamps.

4. How many pencils does Mark buy?
   Mark buys some pencils.

5. How many friends does Jack have?
   Jack has only a few friends.

6. How many pictures are there on the wall?
   There are a few pictures on the wall.

7. Is there much milk in the cup?
   Yes, there is much milk in the cup.

8. Have you got any stamps?
   Yes, I have got some stamps.

UNIT 3

QUANTITY　(II)

♠ 學習目標

讓小朋友學會如何使用 a lot of, many, much 等數量詞, 爲上一課之延續。

♠ 教學方式

(1) 教學方式如 Lesson 2 的(1)。介紹 a lot of, many 和 much。

(2) 小朋友可能會對 some（一些）, many、much（許多）及 a lot of（很多）, a few、a little（幾個）的數量大小, 搞不清楚。可以比大小的方式讓他們了解：a lot of ＞ many（much）＞ some ＞ a few（a little）。

♠ 練　習

(1) 老師先教每位小朋友準備兩張圖卡, 一張畫上可數的名詞數個, 另一張畫上物質名詞。老師每次指定兩位小朋友, 輪流做以下的對話：

B 將 2 張圖片置於胸前, 由 A 問 B。

　A： Are there any ＋ <u>B 圖卡上的可數複數名詞</u> in your picture?

　B： Yes, there are ＋ <u>B 圖卡上的可數名詞</u> in my picture.

　　　*　　　　　　*　　　　　　*

　A： Is there any ＋ <u>B 圖卡上的物質名詞</u> in your picture?

B : Yes, there is 數量詞＋ B 圖卡上的物質名詞 in my
picture.

然後 A、B 互換角色，由 B 問 A 做同樣的對話。

(2) 老師先製作七張圖卡，上面分別寫上 some，any，many，
much，a lot of，a little，a few 等數量詞。再由老師輪流
或點小朋友出來，問他如 p.19 的問題，讓小朋友將數量詞
選出來。答對者才可回座，答錯者則跟著老師將句子唸三
遍。

♠ 教學重點

(1) much（許多）
a little（幾個）　 }　＋不可數名詞

many（許多）
a few（幾個）　 }　＋可數複數名詞

a lot of（很多）
some（一些）
any（任何）　 }　＋可數或不可數名詞

(2) p.21 的 EXERCISE 務必讓小朋友自己做，可於下次上課
時，請小朋友上台來唸自己的造句。

習題解答　**3**-1　**LET'S PRACTICE**（p.19）

Choose the correct one.

1. (a) *much*　　2. (d) *a lot of*　　3. (b) *many*　　4. (a) *any*

5. (c) *much*　　6. (a) *a few*　　7. (c) *some*　　8. (d) *much*

3·3 EXERCISE (p. 21)

Make sentences.

1. **some**

   They have some stamps.

2. **any (negative)**

   I didn't buy any stamps this week.

3. **any (question)**

   Do you have any money ?

4. **a few**

   There are a few pictures on the wall .

5. **a little**

   There is only a little water in the bottle .

6. **a lot of**

   There are a lot of people in the park .

7. **many**

   How many pencils do you have ?

8. **much**

   How much money do you have ?

UNIT 4

THIS IS YOUR DOG, ISN'T IT?

♠ 學習目標

讓小朋友熟練附加問句的用法。

♠ 教學方式

(1) 先向小朋友介紹什麼是附加問句:「當你問完問題時,後面所加上的『不是嗎?』,就是附加問句。」告訴小朋友,若原句是肯定句,則附加問句要用否定,如:This is your dog, isn't it?而若原句是否定句,則附加問句要用肯定,如:This isn't your dog, is it?老師可分①Be 動詞②普通動詞③助動詞三部分來介紹附加問句的改法。

(2) 熟悉本課句型後,老師再帶小朋友唸一段本課會話,請小朋友試著解釋這段會話的意思,再由老師加以修正。然後老師每次指定兩位小朋友上台表演這段會話,直到每個小朋友都扮演過兩個角色後,老師再進行下一段會話。此外要提醒小朋友注意課文中附加問句的地方。

♠ 練 習

(1) 老師每教完一種附加問句的用法(可分①Be 動詞②普通動詞③助動詞三種來教)時,請每位小朋友在圖卡上,自行造句,老師可規定某些學生造現在式,過去式或未來式。然後將這些句子混在一起,每次點一名小朋友出來抽圖卡,就所抽到的句子造附加問句。答錯者則和全班同學一起唸

三遍正確的句子。直到全班都答對了，老師再教下一種附
加問句。

♠ **教學重點**

(1) 附加問句有許多種形式，可分 be 動詞、普通動詞和助動詞
三類，要向小朋友分別解釋清楚，直到小朋友熟練了，再
換下一種形式練習。特別注意，句子若是簡單式時，小朋
友可能無法立即反應，如：He likes Mary, doesn't he?
She bought an apple, didn't she? 若碰到這種情況，
老師應耐心地輔導小朋友，切莫讓小朋友認為英語好難，
而降低興趣。

(2) 否定形式之附加問句須用縮寫形式，注意小朋友對縮寫的
發音。

習題解答

4-1 LET'S PRACTICE （p.24）

Answer questions.

1. *The dog's name is Baby.*

2. *No, Mary's mother doesn't like dogs.*

3. *Yes, Tom takes his dog to the park in the morning.*

4. *Tom takes Baby for a walk in the evening.*

5. *Yes, Baby likes the park.*

6. *Yes, he is very smart.*

7. *Tom washes his dog in the bathroom.*

8. *Yes, I like dogs. (Yes, I do.)*

9. *Yes, I have a dog.*

4-③ EXERCISE (p.26)

Make tag-questions.

(1) *You also like dogs, don't you?*

(2) *He would wash it in the bathroom, wouldn't he?*

(3) *Mark will play baseball tomorrow, won't he?*

(4) *Susan and Paul are good friends, aren't they?*

(5) *She didn't go to school yesterday, did she?*

(6) *He doesn't like to dance, does he?*

(7) *We should do it, shouldn't we?*

(8) *Helen wasn't happy last night, was she?*

UNIT 5

PASSIVE VOICE

♠ 學習目標

讓小朋友學會被動語態的使用：「 be 動詞＋p.p 」，及規則和不規則的動詞三態變化。

♠ 教學方式

(1) 首先用中文向小朋友解釋什麼是主動語態和被動語態。如「我打掃房間。」為主動語態，而「小狗被車子撞到。」則為被動語態。再舉例介紹如何將主動語態改為被動語態的方法。在黑板上寫下：

① I cleaned the room.　改為
（我　打掃　　房間。）

② The room was cleaned by me.
（　房間　　　打掃　　被我。）

第②句的主詞 The room 是被打掃，所以動詞要用被動式「 be 動詞＋p.p.（過去分詞）」的形式。而 by 是「被」之意，後面要接人稱代名詞的受格 “me”。

(2) 告訴小朋友，過去分詞即是我們在 p.28 圖表上所看到的第三列字，而其規則變化是在字尾加上 ed 即可。老師可先利用 p.28 A 部分的單字，在黑板上寫出幾句主動語態的句子，再利用圖表引導小朋友，將這些句子改成被動語態。並可指定小朋友到黑板來練習，老師則個別協助指導。

(3)帶小朋友用韻律的方式，來唸 p.28 B 部分不規則變化的
動詞三態，並指出這些字變化的部分，讓小朋友易於記憶。
之後老師再利用這部分的動詞，在黑板上寫出一些主動語
態的句子，用同樣的方法教小朋友把這些句子改成被動語
態。

(4)老師可利用 p.29 的文章，教小朋友查字典的方法。

♠ 練　習

(1)老師先準備好一些畫著「某人在做某件事」的圖片，儘量先
用以前學過的單字。將小朋友分為兩組，每組輪流派一人
出來抽圖片，先用主動語態來描述圖片，再將它改成被動
語態的句子，答對的小朋友可回組，該組並可得一分。答
錯的小朋友有三次改正的機會，若三次都錯，老師則從旁
協助，並要求這位小朋友把對的句子唸三遍，之後才能回
座，換下一位小朋友出來抽圖片造句。積分多的為優勝隊。

(2)老師可先請每個小朋友回家準備好一張寫著動詞原形的卡
片，將這些卡片交給老師。老師將小朋友分成兩組，每組
每次各派一位代表出來猜拳，贏的人就可以抽卡片，看了
卡片之後再回答這個字的動詞三態，答對則得一分，答錯
則換對方答。若對方也答錯，則由老師解答，若對方答對
則可得原題 2 倍之分數。照這種方式，兩組一直派人輪下
去，最後分數較多的一組為優勝。

♠ 教學重點

(1)本課主動語態的句子改為被動語態的圖表；可視學生程度
予以解說。

主動：主詞＋動詞＋受詞（受格）

被動：受詞（主格）＋ be 動詞＋過去分詞＋ by ＋原主詞（受格）

(2) 本課所列的動詞三態個數頗多，老教應用韻律方式分段教完。

(3) 以後每次上課，都幫小朋友複習動詞三態。

(4) 適度的背誦課文，有助於小朋友熟悉句型觀念。p.27 及 p.29 的文章可讓小朋友背誦，於下次上課時，講他們上來做個小小演說或說故事比賽。

習題解答

5-1 LET'S PRACTICE （p.29）

Read and do.

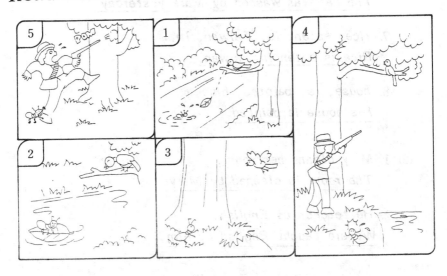

5-③ EXERCISE （p.31）

Rearrange the sentences.

(1) 1. him, English, are, taught, by, we.
<u>We are taught English by him.</u>

2. was, I, made, happy, them, by.
<u>I was made happy by them.</u>

3. Canada, English, spoken, is, in.
<u>English is spoken in Canada.</u>

4. liked, everybody, he, is, by.
<u>He is liked by everybody.</u>

5. every day, cleaned, the classroom, is.
<u>The classroom is cleaned every day.</u>

6. Mark, yesterday, washed, was, the car, by.
<u>The car was washed by Mark yesterday.</u>

7. rice, eaten, is, Taiwan, in.
<u>Rice is eaten in Taiwan.</u>

8. house, is, painted, his.
<u>His house is painted.</u>

(2) 1. Mary cleans her room.   （p.32）
<u>The room is cleaned by Mary.</u>

2. He teaches us English.
<u>We are taught English by him.</u>

3. *A car ran over the dog.*
   The dog was run over by a car.

4. *Mark wrote the letter.*
   The letter was written by Mark.

5. *He closes his store at six.*
   The store is closed by him at six.

6. *Our teachers use this room.*
   This room is used by our teachers.

UNIT 6

RELATIVE PRONOUNS

♠ **學習目標**

讓小朋友學會如何使用關係代名詞 who , which , 和 that 並用它們來造句。

♠ **教學方式**

(1) 老師可先將相關的兩個句子寫在紙片上,將主詞和動詞分開,然後再教小朋友如何將這兩個相關句子用 who , which 或 that 合成一句。以 $\begin{cases} \text{The boy is my brother.} \\ \text{The boy plays tennis.} \end{cases}$ 為例,

紙上則寫上　① The boy　｜ is my brother ｜

　　　　　　② The boy　｜ plays tennis ｜

　　　　　　　who

然後告訴小朋友,如果我們覺得兩個句子太多,而想把它們合成一個句子時,就要變一下魔術,把重覆的 ② The boy 變不見,用 who 取代,再將 who plays tennis 放在 ① The boy 和 is my brother 中間就 O.K. 了。

全句就變成 The boy (who plays tennis) is my brother. (打網球的男孩是我哥哥。)

(2) 注意告訴小朋友 who，which 或 that 一定要放在所重覆的名詞之後，如：

The book ┃ which ┃ I bought is on the desk. 又如：

（取代重覆的 book 。）

Here is a record ┃ which ┃ my father gave me yesterday.

（取代重覆的 record，在這個句子中，which 本來是放在 me 和 yesterday 之間，但要被搬到所取代的 record 之後。）

(3) 老師在敎 which 和 that 時，亦可依照上述的方式，告訴小朋友，主詞是「人」時我們用 who，主詞是「物」時我們用 which，而主詞是「人＋物」時則用 that。

♠ 練　習

(1) 老師先在黑板上，寫出如 p.35 的句子，讓小朋友輪流上來在黑板上用 who，which 或 that 將 2 個句子合爲一句。直到每位小朋友都會爲止。之後，老師改由口頭唸句子的方式，輪流讓小朋友口頭回答，用關係代名詞將 2 個句子合爲一句。

(2) 老師帶小朋友玩「大風吹」的遊戲。老師先替小朋友複習一下遊戲可能會用到的生字，再讓小朋友將椅子面朝外圍成一個圓圈，椅數等於人數減一，小朋友先用猜拳決定誰當 Wind，而 Wind 站在圓圈旁，小朋友則坐在椅子上，Wind 喊："Wind blows..." 其他小朋友則喊："Who do you want to blow？" Wind 則說："I want to blow the persons who～." 一說完後，被吹到的小朋友就要趕

快換位置，而 Wind 也趁機找一個位置坐下，輪到下一個
沒有位置的小朋友當Wind，以同樣的方式進行遊戲。當過
三次Wind 的人就要被罰唱歌或表演。

♠ **教學重點**

(1)本課之基本句型：

①主詞（人）＋<u>who 帶出來之子句</u>＋動詞～。

②主詞（物或事）＋<u>which 帶出來之子句</u>＋動詞～。

③主詞（人＋物）＋<u>that 帶出來之子句</u>＋動詞～。

(2)將兩個相關句子，用關係代名詞合併成一句時，小朋友可
能會發生不知將哪一個句子變成關係子句的困擾，可能會
寫出 The boy who is my brother plays tennis. 的錯誤
句子，此時老師應耐心地予以矯正，讓小朋友多做幾次練
習，並適時予以鼓勵。

(3)本課的who 和 that 之用法，和以前小朋友所學過的不太
一樣，如果「關係代名詞」對他們太難的話，就用「魔術
師」的稱呼來代替。

習題解答

6-1 **LET'S PRACTICE** (p.35)

Look and say.

1. *I know the girl who is playing the guitar.*

2. *I can see a dog which is running along the street.*

3. *I like the story which was written by Mark Twain.*

4. *This is a car which was made in Taiwan.*

5. *Jack who lives in Canada is my friend.*

6. *The cat which is sleeping under the table is "kitty."*

6-2 PLAY A GAME （p.36）

Make a guess.

Jane =(1)
Betty =(2)

6-3 EXERCISE （p.37）

Make sentences.

2. *I know a boy who can draw pictures very well.*

3. *We will visit a girl who was sick yesterday.*

4. *The girl who talked to me was very kind.*

5. *I saw a baby lion which was playing with its mother.*

6. *She had a dog which she loved very much.*

7. *I have an old camera which was given to me by my father.*

UNIT 7

I ENJOY COOKING

♠ 學習目標

讓小朋友熟悉動名詞當主詞的句型，及學會用 like，love，hate，enjoy 等動詞來造句。

♠ 教學方式

(1)告訴小朋友，如果我們要造一個句子：「游泳是我最喜歡的活動。」其中「游泳」是句子中的主詞，但主詞又必須是名詞才行，所以必須把「游泳」(swim)這個動詞變成名詞。變的方法，就是加 ing，成爲 swimming，叫做動名詞，表示由「動詞變來的名詞」。於是句子就是 " Swimming is my favorite activity."

(2)老師帶小朋友大聲唸本課所列舉的動名詞，如：swimming，collecting stamps，playing baseball 等，然後再將它們帶入句子中，並利用圖表向小朋友解釋以動名詞當主詞的句型：

$$\text{動名詞} + \text{is} + \begin{cases} \text{形容詞} \\ \text{名 詞} \end{cases}$$

(3)帶小朋友大聲唸本課以動名詞當主詞的句子，直到他們能自行造句爲止。並利用圖表來介紹下一個句型：

It is ＋形容詞＋ to V.

這種句型是由上一種句型演變而來的，老師可利用以下圖表解釋它們之間的變化情形：

V-ing ＋ is ＋形容詞。

It ＋ is ＋形容詞＋ to V.

並帶小朋友反覆練習這些句子。

(4) 告訴小朋友，一個句子只能有一個「主動詞」，如果要有 2 個動詞，就要用 to 來連接，但第一個動詞還是「主動詞」。如 I go home to sleep.（我回家睡覺。）其中 to sleep 稱為不定詞。讓小朋友利用以前學過的單字，造出有「不定詞」的句子。

(5) 再教小朋友有些特殊動詞如 " like "" love "" hate "等，如果要接動詞時，可接 to ＋ V.，即不定詞的形式，也可接 Ving，即動名詞的形式。但 enjoy 這個動詞，一定要加動名詞。

♠ 練 習

(1) 請小朋友每人畫一張「自己最喜愛的活動」的圖片，老師每次指定兩名小朋友出來，輪流扮演 A、B 角色，做以下的對話：

A : Do you like／enjoy   B圖卡上的活動？

B : Yes, I do. B圖卡上的活動 is my favorite activity.

A : Why do you like／enjoy   B圖卡上的活動？

B：Because B圖卡上的活動 is

> easy.
> interesting.
> good for us.
> （擇任一答）

A：Yes, indeed. It is

> easy
> interesting
> good for us

to B圖卡上的活動 .

(2)老師可先帶領全班小朋友，做下列三個動詞的動作：cooking
（手拿鍋鏟炒菜狀）、swimming（划水狀）、studying
（讀書狀）。然後每次指定兩名小朋友出來，兩人先以剪刀、
石頭、布決定誰來喊拳，贏的小朋友則喊"I enjoy ...
cooking / swimming / studying."同時配合動作，對方若
和這位小朋友做同樣的動作，則輸，回座換下一位小朋友
出來挑戰。但若對方和這位小朋友做不同之動作，則換對
方喊拳，規則同上。最後贏的小朋友則可被封為「拳王」。
老師可再選三個動詞的動作，一直玩下去。

♠ 教學重點

(1)以動名詞當主詞的句子，一律用單數動詞及 be 動詞，老師
在此應提醒小朋友。

(2) love，like，hate 後接不定詞（to＋V）或動名詞（Ving）
的意義相差不大，接不定詞較強調動作，接動名詞較強調
事物。但本課中所提及的 forget 和 stop 後接不定詞和動
名詞的意義就非常不同，一定要使小朋友弄明白這一點。

$$forget + \begin{cases} to\ V. \ (忘記要去做 V.) \\ Ving \ (忘了做過 V.) \end{cases}$$

$$stop + \begin{cases} to\ V. \ (停止而去做 V.) \\ Ving \ (停止做 V.) \end{cases}$$

(3)在 p.41 Tongue twisters 的部分，老師應注意小朋友的
   發音是否正確，以免將來矯正不及。並讓孩子多唸幾次，
   培養他們對英文句子的韻律感。

習題解答　**7-3 EXERCISE** （p.42）

Look and write.

2. *I enjoy playing basketball very much.*
   Playing basketball is my favorite activity.

3. *I enjoy swimming very much.*
   Swimming is my favorite activity.

4. *I enjoy climbing mountains very much*
   Climbing mountains is my favorite activity.

5. *I enjoy camping very much.*
   Camping is my favorite activity.

6. *I enjoy cooking very much.*
   Cooking is my favorite activity.

7. *I enjoy going on a picnic very much.*
   Going on a picnic is my favorite activity.

Look and say. （p.43）

2. *Dancing is very interesting.*

3. *Playing tennis is very interesting.*

4. *Learning English is very interesting.*

Look and write. （p.43）

2. *It began raining.*

3. *My brother likes watching TV.*

4. *They hate going to school on Sunday.*

UNIT 8

IT TASTES GOOD

♠ 教學目標

讓小朋友學會連綴動詞的用法及 not only ～ but also ～的句型。

♠ 教學方式

(1) 老師先利用圖片及動作，帶小朋友大聲唸本課所列出的連綴動詞 look beautiful，taste good，smell delicious 等。待小朋友明白這些連綴動詞的意思後，再將它們帶入課文中的句子，由老師帶讀，小朋友邊看圖邊讀以了解課文的意思。並用以下圖表讓學生了解本課的句型：

> 主詞＋連綴動詞＋形容詞。
> 主詞＋連綴動詞＋ like（像）＋名詞。

老師可利用課本的句子及自己舉例讓小朋友練習，直到他們能夠自己造句為止。

(2) 向小朋友解釋 and（和）和 but（但是）意思之不同，及其用法之差別，然後再解釋 not only ～ but also ～（不但～，而且～）之意義及其用法。老師可利用 p.46 的圖案和句子來讓小朋友練習，直到他們熟練這種句型為止。

♠ 練 習

(1) 請小朋每人用連綴動詞造一個句子，並寫在圖卡上，再自己上插圖。上課時，老師每次指定兩位小朋友，根據自己的圖卡做下面的對話：

    A：How do you like   B圖片上的物品?

    B：I like it very much. It 連綴動詞＋形容詞 .
        And how do you like   A圖片上的物品?

    A：I like it very much. It 連綴動詞＋形容詞 .

(2)老師先準備一個紙箱子，在箱子上打一個讓小朋友的手能
伸進箱子的洞，然後請小朋友從家裏帶一件玩具或任何不
容易摸出是什麼東西的物品，放入箱中。將小朋友分成兩
組，兩組輪流派一人出來，將手伸進箱內，拿一物品，先
說：" It feels like 某物品 . "，然後再將物品拿出箱外，
若這位小朋友猜對他所拿的物品，則可得分，猜錯則不得
分，回座後再換下一位小朋友出來猜箱中之物品。最後由
得分較多的那組優勝。

♠ **教學重點**

(1) both ～ and ～ 及 not only ～ but also ～ 所連接的是同樣
詞性的東西，例如同樣是名詞或同是動詞片語，老師應解
釋清楚，並注意小朋友有沒有用錯。

習題解答 **8-1 LET'S PRACTICE** （p.46）

Look and say.

1. *The cat is not only fat but also ugly.*

2. *Tom not only read the book but also saw the movie.*

3. *Jane not only wrote a letter but also cleaned her room.*

4. *The cake not only smells good but also tastes good.*

*   *   *

1. *The cake tastes delicious.*

2. *Mary looks nice.*

3. *The milk tastes sour.*

4. *The story sounds interesting.*

8-③ EXERCISE (p.48)

Answer questions.

(1) *It looks bad.*

(2) *I feel tired.*

(3) *It looks like a ball.*

(4) *It tastes delicious.*

(5) *The music sounds sweet.*

(6) *It tastes like beef.*

(7) *It sounds exciting.*

(8) *It smells fresh.*

UNIT 9

SOUR GRAPES

♠ **學習目標**

讓小朋友學會 so～that 及 too～to 的用法，並能用它們來造句。

♠ **教學方式**

(1)本課也是要教小朋友將 2 個句子變成一個句子的方法。首先在黑板上寫下：

You're very late.　　　你遲到了。

You can't take the bus. 你無法趕上公車。

告訴小朋友，這 2 句話可以變成「你太晚了而無法趕上公車」，其中「太～而不能～」用" too～to ～來造句：

You're <u>too late to take the bus</u>.

(2)介紹 <u>too＋形容詞＋ to ＋原形動詞</u>之後，讓小朋友先用中文說出幾個「太～而不能～」的句子，如「太老了而不能走路」、「太忙而不能來」等，再由老師協助，將這些中文翻成英文：" too old to walk"，"too busy to come"，待小朋友都會了之後，再加入主詞成為完整句子，由老師帶讀。

(3)用同樣的方法先讓小朋友練習造 <u>so＋形容詞＋ that＋句子</u>（如此～以致於～）的英文詞語，熟練之後，再加入完整句子。注意 that 後面要接完整的句子。

(4)老師先一段一段地帶讀課文，並解釋較難的句子，講解完
　　後，老師可讓小朋友每兩人一組出來表演，一人唸著課文，
　　另一人則依課文來表演狐狸。

♠ 練　習

(1)小朋友圍成一個圓圈，老師以輪流或點名的方式，叫一名
　　小朋友出來，用 too～to～或 so～that～來造句，若造
　　對句子，則由老師作一手勢，全班齊喊：" You are so
　　great that you can do it."這位小朋友就可回座。若小
　　朋友造錯句子，可有兩次更正機會，若兩次皆錯，則須被
　　罰唱歌，並重覆一次對的句子，才可回座。

(2)老師將許多如 p.50 的兩個相關句子寫在圖畫紙上，並將它
　　們分開，分給每個小朋友一人一句，另外再將解釋兩個相
　　關句子的圖片貼在黑板上。讓小朋友根據圖片自行尋找自
　　己的相關句子，然後兩人共同用 too～to～或 so～that～
　　將兩個句子連接起來，再跑到黑板前將解釋這句話的圖片
　　拿下來，連同改造過的句子交給老師。完全做對且最迅速
　　的一組為優勝。最後一名要出來表演。

♠ 教學重點

(1)提醒學生有些句子如 { John is very busy.　He can't go to the party. }

　　這 2 句，可以用「too～to～」，也可以用「so～that
　　～」來接合：

　　① John is too busy to go to the party.

　　② John is so busy that he can't go to the party.

(2)本課課文中有牽涉到過去完成式（ the most beautiful grapes he had ever seen.）及使役動詞（ they made his mouth water.）之用法。老師稍微解釋一下即可，後面幾課還會再提到，屆時亦可翻回來解說。

習題解答

9-1 LET'S PRACTICE （p.50）

Look and say.

1. *The question is too difficult for us to answer.*

2. *My father is too busy to watch TV.*

3. *The man was too old to drive a car.*

*　　　　*　　　　*

1. *She was so scared that she could not move.*

2. *It is so cold that I can't go out.*

3. *I was so sick that I could not go to school.*

9-3 EXERCISE （p.52）

Change the sentences with "so ~ that".

1. *Jack was so thirsty that he couldn't study.*

2. *The tea is so hot that I can't drink it.*

3. *I was so shy that I could not speak in public.*

4. The driver was so busy that he couldn't come.

5. I was so late that I couldn't watch the cartoon.

6. The question is so difficult that he can't answer it.

7. He is so old that he can't dance.

Join the two sentences with "so ~ that" or "too ~ to". (p.53)

1. It's so noisy that you can't sleep well near an airport.

2. Your brother is too young to go to school.

3. The question is too difficult for him to answer.

4. He spoke so fast that I couldn't understand him.

5. I was too late to catch the bus.

6. The book was so interesting that I read it many times.

7. The tea is too hot for me to drink.

UNIT 10

HOW TERRIBLE！

♠ 學習目標

讓小朋友學會如何將直述句改爲感歎句，以及感官動詞和使役動詞的用法。

♠ 教學方式

(1)老師先在黑板上寫一些直述句，然後詢問小朋友，如果要強調這句話的語氣時該怎麼辦。接著就用圖表介紹感歎句的構造及直述句變成感歎句的改法：

Ⓐ 主詞＋（be）動詞＋形容詞。

→ How＋形容詞＋主詞＋（be）動詞。

John is very hungry.
→ How hungry John is.

Ⓑ 主詞＋be 動詞＋名詞。

→What＋名詞＋主詞＋be 動詞。

It is a very tall tree.
→What a tall tree it is.

老師可在黑板上寫出直述句，讓小朋友上來改感嘆句。

(2) 老師帶小朋友讀課文會話，然後再輪流指定三位小朋友出來表演 Mom，Dad 和 John 的角色，直到每位小朋友都演過每個角色為止。

(3) 前面第 7 課曾敎過「不定詞」的用法，在黑板上寫出例句先幫小朋友複習不定詞。

(4) 再介紹「使役動詞」make，let 和「感官動詞」watch，hear，see，feel 等的中文意義。告訴小朋友這些動詞，如果後面要加動詞時，就直接用<u>動詞原形</u>，如 She <u>watched</u> us <u>play</u>（動詞原形）in the park. 利用本課的圖片和例句，多帶小朋友跟讀。

♠ 練　習

(1) 老師可先準備一些如 p.58 A 部分的圖片並寫上關鍵形容詞，將小朋友分為兩組，將這些圖片分別置於兩組的桌前，兩組輪流派出一位小朋友上前抽圖片，根據圖片內容來造一感歎句，答對的小朋友可回座，然後換下一位同學出來抽圖片造句。而造錯句子的小朋友有兩次更正機會，若兩次皆不對，則由老師協助，造正確句子，老師並要求此位小朋友將正確句子唸三遍，之後才能換下一位小朋友出來抽圖片造句。先輪完的那組即為優勝。

(2) 老師將 watch，make，hear，let，see，feel，help 分別寫在七張圖卡上，面朝下放在講桌上，小朋友則圍成一個圓圈，由老師帶小朋友唱一首英文歌，並拿一枝原子筆，邊唱邊傳。歌唱完時，拿到筆的小朋友就必須出來抽圖卡，用上面的動詞，造一個句子。答對的話，由老師帶全班一起喊 "What a good student you are." 然後再繼續玩。

答錯的小朋友則出局，到旁邊去。最後，答錯的小朋友們要一起表演一個節目。

♠ 教學重點

(1) help 的用法較特別，它接動詞時，可用「不定詞」（ to ＋ V. ），也可接原形動詞。如 He helped us <u>to cook</u>. or He helped us <u>cook</u>.

(2) 小朋友在造感嘆句時，可能無法立即反應，老師應耐心地指導他們，給小朋友充分的時間多練習。

 習題解答

10-1 LET'S PRACTICE （ p.56 ）

Look and say.

1. *What beautiful flowers she has !*

2. *What a nice party it was !*

3. *What bad grades they are !*

* * *

1. *How interesting the book is !*

2. *How tall Paul is !*

3. *How sad Nancy was !*

10-③ **EXERCISE** (p.58)

Make sentences.

A 2. *How old the book is !*

3. *How glad Nancy is !*

4. *How pretty Mary is !*

6. *What a kind girl (she is) !*

7. *What a small radio (it is) !*

8. *What a beautiful flower (it is) !*

B 2. *We make Nancy happy.*

3. *I hear Mary sing a song.*

4. *Father doesn't let me watch TV .*

5. *I see the dog run away.*

6. *I felt the ground move.*

7. *I help my mother clean the room.*

UNIT 11

EITHER & NEITHER

♠ 學習目標

讓小朋友學會 either ～ or ～ 及 neither ～ nor ～的句型，和 I do, too. 及 I don't, either. 的倒裝句法。

♠ 教學方式

(1) 在黑板上寫下：He has a new car, and I <u>have a new car, too</u>. 並用黃色粉筆在 have a new car 下面畫線。告訴小朋友「 too 」是「也」的意思，而且黃線部分的意思和前半句重複，為求簡潔起見，重複的地方可用一個助動詞來代替。於是就變成：He has a new car, and I do, too.

(2) 老師在黑板上寫幾個例句，請小朋友上來改成 I do, too. 或 I did, too. 的句子。然後帶讀，直到小朋友能口頭馬上反應為止。

(3) 教小朋友如何將 I do, too. 改為倒裝句：將 too 改為 so，再全句倒過來，即成 So do I. 讓小朋友用黑板上的例句來改倒裝句。

(4) 同如上的方法，介紹 either 及 neither (nor) 的用法。

(5) 先幫小朋友複習 not only ～, but also ～的句型，再介紹 either ～ or ～ (不是～就是～) 及 neither ～ nor ～ (不

是～也不是～）。舉例告訴小朋友它們之後都必須接同性質的東西才公平，如 2 邊都接動詞或接名詞才行。

♠ 練　習

(1) 每 4 個人一組，按高矮排好。每組都要到老師面前來，做倒裝句的練習。由第一位小朋友造一個句子，如 " I have a new car." 然後到第四位小朋友後面蹲下。原來的第 2 位小朋友則用助動詞造 I do, too 或 I don't either. 的句子，如 " <u>第一位小朋友的名字</u> has a new car, and I do, too." 然後再到原來第一位小朋友後面蹲下，原來第三位小朋友則造倒裝句：" <u>第一位小朋友的名字</u> has a new car. So do I." 然後也跑到最後面蹲下。原來第四位小朋友，再重新造一個句子，重頭開始，一直到每位小朋友都練習過每一種句型爲止。

(2) 老師先在紙條上寫上 either ～ or ～和 neither ～ nor ～ 的句子，紙條數要和班上同學一樣多。然後放到紙箱中。將小朋友分爲 2 組，分別派一人上來抽紙條，玩「比手劃腳」的遊戲，表演的人不能說話，只能用動作讓隊友猜所抽到的句子。計時 10 分鐘，答對最多的爲優勝。

♠ 教學重點

(1) 本課內容較多，可分爲三次授完。儘量讓學生從不斷的練習中，自然反應。

(2) 在教 I do, too. 或 I don't, either. 時，告訴小朋友助動詞 do, does, did 是代替普通動詞，如 have, take, buy 等。若是 be 動詞或助動詞 can, should 等的話，就保留 be 動詞或原助動詞即可，如：

I <u>am</u>, too. He <u>is not</u>, either.

I <u>can</u>, too. He <u>can't</u>, either.

(3) 在教 either ～ or ～ 及 neither ～ nor ～ 之前，可幫學生復
習以前教過的動詞，如 ride a bicycle, take a taxi 等。

習題解答 **11·1 LET'S PRACTICE**（p.61）

Look and say.

1. *You can either eat at a restaurant or cook at home.*

2. *You can buy either a sweater or a shirt.*

3. *You can eat either a hamburger or noodles.*

4. *You can either ride a bicycle or take a taxi.*

5. *You can choose either a magazine or a dictionary.*

*　　　　*　　　　*（p.62）

1. *Nancy wants neither a skirt nor a sweater.*

2. *Helen neither drank coffee nor ate any hamburgers.*

3. *Bill can neither sing nor ride a bicycle very well.*

4. *Tom is neither tall nor fat.*

5. *John likes to order neither a coke nor a milk shake.*

11-③ EXERCISE （p. 64）

Look and write.

Ⓐ 2. *So am I.*
   I am, too.

4. *Neither am I.*
   I am not, either.

3. *Neither do I.*
   I don't, either.

5. *Neither did I.*
   I didn't, either.

Ⓑ 2. *Bill drinks neither coffee nor milk.*

3. *Either Peter or Wayne will go fishing.*

4. *My father orders either hamburgers or fried chicken.*

5. *Neither Susan nor Nancy swept the floor.*

6. *Wayne wants either a bicycle or a car.*

7. *Peter can neither sing a song nor ride a bicycle.*

8. *Helen can either sing or dance.*

UNIT 12

I HAVE READ IT

♠ 學習目標

讓小朋友複習動詞三態變化。熟悉現在完成式（has）have
＋p.p. 的句型，並能利用現在完成式造句。

♠ 教學方式

(1)老師先幫小朋友複習動詞三態變化，特別是不規則的變化。

(2)介紹現在完成式，告訴小朋友主要的變化在<u>動詞</u>部分：

$$主詞 + \left. \begin{matrix} have \\ has \end{matrix} \right\} + 過去分詞$$

（動詞）

然後先帶小朋友大聲唸 have read，has read，have lived，
has lived 等詞語，待小朋友習慣之後，再將這些詞語帶
入句子中，老師帶讀句子，小朋友則大聲跟讀。

(3)小朋友熟練 have（has）＋p.p. 的句型之後，再加上表時
間的副詞，如 for a long time，for two years，many
times 等。

(4)告訴小朋友改疑問句時，只要把 have 或 has 搬到句首即
可。此時的 have 或 has 相當於 do，does，did 等助動詞，
因此回答時也可用 Yes，I have 或 No，I haven't. 來簡
答。

♠ 練 習

　(1) 以分組比賽的方式為小朋友複習動詞三態變化。老師先在
　　　紙片上寫上所學過動詞的原形，放入紙箱中。將全班分為
　　　二組，每次各派一位上來，互相猜拳，贏的人可抽紙條，
　　　並說出那個動詞的三態變化，答對則得一分。答錯則對方
　　　可搶答，對方答對的話，對方可得 2 分，若對方也答錯，
　　　則雙方平手，都不得分。再換另一組上來猜拳抽籤，直到
　　　每個人都上來過為止。得分多的為優勝組，最後由老師將
　　　2 組都不會的動詞三態講解一遍。

　(2) 讓每位小朋友用「現在完成式」造一個句子，寫在圖畫紙
　　　上，掛在胸前，大家圍一個圓圈，從左到右把自己的句子
　　　唸一遍。然後老師走到一個學生 A 面前看的句子，問他：
　　　Have you ever ＋ A 的過去分詞？ A 則回答 "Yes, I have."
　　　或 "No, I haven't." 然後老師再指著任一學生 B 的句子
　　　問 A：Has B ever ＋ B 的過去分詞？ A 則根據 B 的句子
　　　作答。之後換 B 出來當老師的角色，走到任一學生面前問
　　　問題，不可叫重複的人，直到每位小朋友都出來過為止。

　(3) 程度較佳的班上，可讓小朋友輪流上台演講自己的一次旅
　　　遊經歷，包括旅遊的地點、搭乘的交通工具、旅遊的時間
　　　及當時的天氣，並可簡單地敍述旅途中發生的趣事。小朋
　　　友在描述時可能會發生詞彙不足的困擾，老師可在旁協助。
　　　講完之後，台下的小朋友亦可對演講內容發問。

♠ 教學重點

　(1) 注意 already，ever，yet，just 等表時間的副詞在句中的
　　　位置。

① 主詞 + $\begin{cases} \text{have} \\ \text{has} \end{cases}$ + $\begin{cases} \text{already} \\ \text{just} \end{cases}$ + p.p.

② $\begin{cases} \text{Has} \\ \text{Have} \end{cases}$ + 主詞 + ever + p.p. ?

③ $\begin{cases} \text{Has} \\ \text{Have} \end{cases}$ + 主詞 + p.p. + $\begin{cases} \text{already} \\ \text{yet} \end{cases}$?

不要讓小朋友死記這些句型，而要用不斷反覆的帶讀練習，讓他們自然而然的記住。

(2)雖然 read 的三態同形，但其過去式及過去分詞都唸〔rɛd〕。

(3)可試著向小朋友解釋「現在完成式」在時間上的意義，表示到現在為止。

習題解答 **12-1 LET'S PRACTICE** （p.69）

Look and say.

1. A : *How long have you studied English?*
   B : *I've studied English for two years.*

2. A : *How long have you been sick?*
   B : *I've been sick for a long time.*

3. A : *How long have you stayed in the U.S.A.?*
   B : *I've stayed in the U.S.A. for three years.*

＊　　　　＊　　　　＊

A : *Have you decided what to do this winter?*

You : *Yes, I plan to go skiing.*

A : *That's great. I've never gone skiing before.*

You : *What are you going to do this winter?*

A : *I want to have a trip to America but I don't have money.*

12-③   **EXERCISE** (p. 71)

Make sentences.

2. *They have lived in Taiwan for a long time.*

3. *My brother has washed the car for two hours.*

4. *He has been sick for a long time.*

5. *I have just opened all the windows.*

6. *I have already finished my homework.*

7. *My mother and father haven't come home yet.*

8. *He has visited Europe several times.*

9. *Have you ever seen that movie?*

UNIT 13

WHAT WOULD YOU DO?

♠ 學習目標

教小朋友學會由 if 所帶領的假設句和條件句，並了解其中的差別。

♠ 教學方式

(1) 先向小朋友舉例說明用到 if（如果）的情形有 2 種。第一種是表示未來，有可能實現的「條件句」，如「如果明天不下雨，我們就去爬山。」「如果你也去，我就去。」等都是。第二種是表示與現在事實相反的「假設句」，如「假如我是一隻小鳥，我就能飛。」「假如我有錢，我就去環遊世界。」等，而事實上我不是一隻鳥，我也沒有錢。

(2) 介紹有可能實現的「條件句」：

If + 現在式，主詞 + will + 原形動詞

→ If the weather is fine, we will go picnicking.

(3) 叫每個小朋友用中文造一個「條件句」，再由老師協助寫成英文。全班都會寫了之後，由老師用中文造句，讓小朋友口頭翻成英文。

(4) 同(2)(3)的方式介紹與現在事實相反的「假設句」：

If + 過去式，主詞 + $\begin{cases} \text{would , could} \\ \text{might , should} \end{cases}$ + 原形動詞

If the weather were fine, we would go picnicking.

♠ 練　習

(1) 老師先讓每位小朋友在心裡想好，如果周末天氣很好的話，他們想做些什麼。然後小朋友按身高排成一直綫，由老師問第一個小朋友："What are you going to do this weekend ?"，第一個小朋友則回答" If the weather is fine, I will ～ ."回答正確之後，由他問下一個小朋友同一個問題，如此一直輪流問下去。回答不出來的小朋友，由老師協助。

(2) 以同樣的方式，練習

　　A： If you had one million dollars, what would you do?

　　B： If I had one million dollars, I would ～ .

的句型。

♠ 教學重點

(1) If 條件句的基本句型：

「If ＋現在式，～ will ＋原形動詞」表示未來可能實現的事實。

(2) If 假設句的基本句型：

「If ＋過去式，～ $\begin{cases} \text{would} \\ \text{could} \\ \text{might} \\ \text{should} \end{cases}$ ＋原形動詞」

表示不可能實現，或與現在相反的事實。其中 If 帶出的句子中，be 動詞一律用 " were "。

習題解答 13-1 LET'S PRACTICE （p. 73）

Look and say.

A̅ 1. *If I had time, I would do my homework.*

2. *If we had a holiday, we could go camping.*

3. *If I were rich, I could travel around the world.*

4. *If Jack took off his coat, he would catch a cold.*

5. *If I had a dictionary, I could look up the word.*

6. *If I were a bird, I could fly.*

B̅ 1. *If Peter finishes his work, he will go to the party.*

2. *If the movie is popular, they will go to see the movie.*

3. *If Susan is sick, she will stay home and rest.*

4. *If Jack studies hard, he will get good grades.*

5. *If the weather is fine, they will go on a picnic.*

6. *If they go to the beach, they will wear swimming suits.*

13-③ **EXERCISE** (p. 76)

Make sentences.

Ⓐ 1. *If I have time, I will write to you.*

2. *If my brother has a car, he will drive to school.*

3. *If we have a holiday, we will go camping in the mountains.*

4. *If he has some money, he will buy a new bicycle.*

5. *If you are rich, you will go around the world.*

6. *If she knows, she will tell about it.*

7. *If you take off your coat, you will catch a cold.*

8. *If I go to the party, I will tell you.*

Ⓑ 1. *If I had time, I would write to you.*

2. *If my brother had a car, he would drive to school.*

3. *If we had a holiday, we would go camping in the mountains.*

4. *If he had some money, he would buy a new bicycle.*

5. *If you were rich, you would go around the world.*

6. *If she knew, she would tell about it.*

7. *If you took off your coat, you would catch a cold.*

8. *If I went to the party, I would tell you.*

第 五 冊 學 習 內 容 一 覽 表

單元	內　　　容	練　　　習	活　　　動	習　　作
複習第四冊	(1) A.我星期一來 B.你的生日是什麼時候？ (2) 誰最胖？ (3) 我昨天打網球 (4) 我將唸英文	Look and read. Look and say. Look and say. Look and say. Look and say.		
1	瑪麗是個好女孩 總是、通常和經常	Look and say：看圖練習各種頻率副詞，如 always, usually, often 等的用法。	韻律：Listen to Me.	Rearrange the sentences.
2	數　量 ㈠	Read and match：利用連連看練習 some, a little, any, a few 等。	遊戲：What am I doing？	Answer questions.
3	數　量 ㈡	Choose the correct one：利用選擇題複習 a lot of, many, much 及前面敘過的數量形容詞。	歌曲：If you are happy.	Make sentences.
4	這是你的狗，不是嗎？	Answer questions：口說練習，造附加問句。	遊戲：Get the apple.	Make tag-questions.
5	被動態 動詞三態	Read and do：閱讀一段短文故事，將圖片重新組合。	歌曲：Looby Loo	Rearrange the sentences.
6	關係代名詞 who, which 和 that	Look and say：從圖片中練習將2個句子用關係代名詞連接起來。	遊戲：Make a guess.	Make sentences.
7	我喜歡烹飪	Look and read：列出動名詞當主詞及 like, love, hate, enjoy 等動詞的句型。	遊戲：Tongue twisters.	Look and write. Look and say. Look and write.
8	嚐起來很好吃	Look and say：練習 not only～, but also～ 及連綴動詞如 feel, sound, taste 等接形容詞的句型。	歌曲：Edelweiss	Answer questions.
9	酸葡萄	Look and say：看圖練習 so～that 及 too～to 的句型。	歌曲：Sing	Change the sentences. Join the sentences.
10	多可怕！ 感官動詞和使役動詞	Look and say：看圖練習用 how 和 what 造感嘆句。	遊戲：Make a paper crane.	Make sentences.
11	either 和 neither 我也是	Look and say：看圖練習造 either ～or～，及 neither～nor～ 的句型。	歌曲：Do - Re - Mi.	Look and write.
12	我已經讀過了 美國之旅	Look and say：2人一組，看圖練習現在完成式的問答對話。 Say and write：告訴同伴你的寒假計劃。	遊戲：Who did what？	Make sentences.
13	你會怎麼辦？	Look and say：看圖練習條件式的假設句及與現在事實相反的假設句。	歌曲：Donna Donna	Make sentences.
複習	(1) 不規則動詞三態表 (2) 口說練習 (3) 歌曲	Answer questions. It's a small world.		

Let's Start with English

習題解答

Review 1 ⟩ **My Hobby** （p.1）

Look and read.

My Hobby

Name: John **Grade:** 6 **Date:** 2/24

My hobby is <u>collecting stamps</u>. <u>Collecting stamps</u> is interesting. I **like** <u>looking at</u> my stamps with my <u>friends</u>.

I **began** <u>collecting stamps</u> when I was in the third grade. My <u>father</u> gave <u>me</u> all his stamps at that time, because he was **so** busy **that** he didn't have time to collect them.

My <u>stamps</u> come from many countries. They **look beautiful**. I **enjoy learning** about different countries this way.

Review 2	**Passive Voice &** **Relative Pronouns** (p. 2)

Make sentences.

(1) 1. *The dress was made by Susan.*

  2. *The car was washed by Wayne.*

  3. *The book was written by Mary's uncle.*

  4. *The wall was painted by Tom.*

(2) 1. *The girl who is playing tennis is my sister.*

  2. *The book which I bought yesterday is on the desk.*

  3. *The cookies which were made by Mary are delicious.*

  4. *I know the boy who can draw pictures very well.*

  5. *We will visit the girl who is in the hospital.*

  6. *This is the car which is made in the R.O.C.*

UNIT 1

A NEW SCHOOL YEAR

♠ 教學目標

讓小朋友學會如何用英語做自我介紹及用英文填寫個人的基本資料。

♠ 教學方式

(1) 直接向小朋友點明，本課的主旨是要用英語做自我介紹。先問小朋友，用英語介紹自己時要介紹些什麼，然後把小朋友所提出來的項目寫在黑板上，並加上本課所提出之項目，在每一項目後列舉例句，由老師帶讀，小朋友跟讀。

(2) 老師先帶讀課文會話，解釋完課文之後，再教小朋友輪流上台表演Mr. Wang，而依照同學的名字來問課文所提出的問題。直到每個人都表演過Mr. Wang之後，老師可再帶讀p.7的三則自我介紹的範例，並教小朋友如何填寫p.8的自我資料。

(3) 老師檢查過每一個小朋友所填寫的自我資料無誤之後，再教小朋友將自己的基本資料代入 p.10 的練習中，試著用這些句子來熟悉自我介紹的方式，當然小朋友在做自我介紹時，還可以加進自己其他的特點或經歷。

♠ 練 習

(1) 老師可請每一位小朋友拿著 p.8 填好的表格輪流上台介紹自己，然後老師問台下的小朋友有關這位小朋友自我介紹的內容。

(2)由老師設計一篇自我介紹的稿子，並按照內容做好如p.8
　　的表格，影印給每位小朋友，然後由老師上台做這篇自我
　　介紹，讓小朋友用聽寫的方式，填好這張表格。完全填正
　　確的小朋友可給予文具、糖果等獎品。

(3)請小朋友回家準備一篇自我介紹的稿子，小朋友可以選各
　　種人物來做自我介紹，假裝自己是電影名星、歌星、卡通
　　人物等。下次上課時，讓每位小朋友上來發表。也可以將
　　名字先略去，讓台下的小朋友聽完後猜猜看，自我介紹的
　　人物是誰。

♠ **教學重點**

(1)從本冊開始，將復習前面五冊的重要句型、單字。因此較
　　著重小朋友的整合閱讀能力及讓小朋友將句型應用到日常
　　會話中。

```
───────── 本課重要單字、片語 ─────────

• past          • special         • several
• sure          • such as ～       • program
• yourselves    • interest        • subject
• greeting      • how about ～     • least
• else          • almost
• important     • go ahead
```

1-1 LET'S PRACTICE （p.8）

Look and write.

Something about myself

Put your photo here.

Name: Susan Wang

Age: twelve

Birthday: May fifth

Elementary School: Chung Shan

Grade: Sixth

Hobbies: singing , dancing

Favorite sport: volleyball

Favorite music: pop music

Favorite TV program: Cosby Show

Favorite food: chocolate cake

Favorite subject: English   Natural Science

Least favorite subject: Math

1-③ EXERCISE (p.10)

Hello. How are you? My name is _____Tom_____ . I am
_____twelve_____ years old. My birthday is on _____November_____
_____first_____ . I go to _____Chung Shan_____ Elementary School.
I'm in the _____sixth_____ grade. I have several hobbies.
One of them is _____singing_____ . My favorite sport is
_____baseball_____ . My favorite TV program is _____McGyver_____ .
I like to eat _____fried chicken_____
(**food**) very much.

_____Math_____ (**subject**) is
my favorite school
subject. I am going to
be a (an) _____teacher_____
when I grow up.
Thank you.

UNIT 2

A BIRTHDAY PRESENT

♠ 教學目標

利用溫馨有趣的故事，培養小朋友閱讀的耐心，並複習未來式 be going to 的句型及動詞過去式的用法。

♠ 教學方式

(1) 先幫小朋友複習未來式 will 及 be going to 的句型，包括肯定句、否定句及疑問句。

(2) 讓小朋友把課本翻到 p.70～71 兩頁，將這些不規則動詞的過去式記牢。再為他們舉例複習過去式的肯定句、否定句及疑問句。

(3) 老師逐段帶讀課文，並逐段解釋課文內容，注意速度儘量放慢。整個課文講解完後，老師可參考 p.12 下面的問題，來問小朋友，確定小朋友是否懂課文內容的意思。然後再讓小朋友四人一組，一人旁白，三人演劇中角色，給小朋友半堂課的時間練習，然後一組一組上台表演，表演得好的小組可得到老師的獎勵。

♠ 練 習

(1) 老師將 p.70、p.71 兩頁上的動詞原形分別寫在一張張圖卡上面，蓋在桌上，然後點名或輪流請小朋友上來，一次抽三張圖卡，並背出動詞三態變化；三個都答對，才可回座，答錯的小朋友，下次上課再上來抽背。

(2) 讓小朋友用未來式寫 10 句左右，關於這個星期日要做什麼事，一個個上來報告。在台下的小朋友要將同學們要做的事記下來，輪完之後，由老師抽問。

(3) 利用(2)的方式，請小朋友寫下 10 句左右，上個星期六做了些什麼事。每個小朋友報告完了之後，老師可指出小朋友是否有錯誤的句子或糾正發音。

♠ 教學重點

(1) 從本課開始，每課課文的長度皆比前五冊的長，老師應利用課文的故事性，配合小朋友的表演活動，使小朋友不會厭煩長課文的閱讀。

(2) 提醒小朋友過去式規則變化中，字尾加 ed 時的發音。（請參考第 4 冊第 8 課教師手冊的教學重點。）

── 本課重要單字、片語 ──

- marry
- die（died died）
- himself
- pass
- pocket
- enough

- pay for
- different
- take a picture
- photo
- bless
- of course

2-1 LET'S PRACTICE (p.13)

(1) Look and say.

1. Helen is going to call Mark.

2. They are going to play baseball.

3. Susan is going to ride a bicycle with Mary and Helen.

4. Peter is going to do his homework.

(2) Choose the correct words.

Words for you: funny animals came pictures zoo lunch joined stood took was

Yesterday Tom and I went to the (zoo).

I took some (pictures) of Tom with different kinds of (animals). When we had (lunch) on the grass, some girl students (joined) us. I (took) a picture of them with Tom.

But when it (came) out, Tom (was) surprised to find that a monkey (stood) between the girls and him.

He looks like a father monkey and this makes this photo look (funny).

2-③ EXERCISE (p.15)

Fill in the blanks.

A

1. He __washed__ the car last Sunday. (**wash**)
2. They __went__ to the library last week. (**go**)
3. __were__ Jane and Nancy busy yesterday? (**are**)
4. Tom __studied__ English three years ago. (**study**)
5. My father __gave__ me a pretty dog last year. (**give**)
6. Mr. Smith __liked__ cats when he was young. (**like**)
7. Jane and Mary __visited__ Taipei two years ago. (**visit**)
8. There __was__ a library in this city last year. (**is**)
9. His uncle __had__ two dogs in his house last year. (**has**)
10. __Was__ English difficult for you when you were a child? (**is**)
12. Our class __began__ at 8:30 last Wednesday. (**begin**)
13. __Did__ your mother __buy__ a book for you? (**buy**)

B

1. I __will__ write a letter this evening.
2. Ben __will__ __be__ free tomorrow.
3. I am __going__ to study Math.
4. __Will__ Tom get up at seven tomorrow?
5. Helen __is__ __going__ to listen to the radio after dinner.

UNIT 3

ASKING THE WAY

♠ 教學目標

讓小朋友練習用英語來問路及為別人指路，並複習「數量形容詞」及「頻率副詞」。

♠ 教學方式

(1) 老師在上這一課時，可以請小朋友把第五冊一起帶來，老師可利用第五冊一、二、三課的圖片和句子，帶小朋友一邊看圖、一邊跟讀，來複習「數量形容詞」和「頻率副詞」的句型。然後再讓小朋友做 p.20 的題目，使他們能夠熟練。

(2) 先在黑板上用圖形解釋問路時的重要語句。如

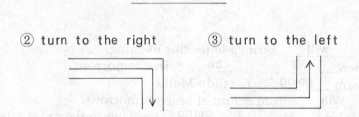

① keep going

② turn to the right　③ turn to the left

(3) 老師逐段帶讀課文之對話，並逐段解釋內容，每解釋完一段，就將小朋友分成兩組，一組扮演一個角色，練習對話，然後再交換角色。整個課文講解完之後，老師再讓每兩個小朋友為一組，練習對話，十五分鐘之後，再讓每組小朋友輪流出來抽籤，決定表演那一則對話。

♠ **練　習**

(1) 老師先點 4 名小朋友上台來當老板，其它小朋友每 4 個人
一組當顧客。老師再將事先寫好的圖卡平均分給各組，或
請各組派代表上來抽卡。(老師在圖卡上要寫上如 some
milk, a lot of books, a few pencils 等數量形容詞加可
數或不可數名詞。)告訴每組小朋友將抽到的圖卡上的東
西記下來，這就是他們那組的購物單。然後再將圖卡收回
來，隨機分給台上的 4 位老板。老板不能讓顧客看到他店
裡有什麼東西。然後每組小朋友開始分頭去購物，把圖卡
買回來，並和老板做以下的對話：

　　老板：May I help you?

　　顧客：I want to buy ＿＿＿＿＿.

　　老板：Yes. I have ＿＿＿＿＿. Here you are./
　　　　　or I'm sorry. I don't have ＿＿＿＿＿.

　各組比賽，哪一組最先買完即優勝。

(2) 老師先準備多張紙條，上面用英文寫上一些指示路線的用
語，如 " keep going for two blocks." " Turn to the
right at the second corner." " Go back for three
blocks." 等，放到紙箱中。然後在黑板上畫一個如 p.18
目的街道圖，越複雜越好。在上面設定 2、3 個目的地，
把學生分成 2 組，每次派一人上台來猜拳，贏的可抽紙條，
並用粉筆根據紙條的指示畫路線，看哪一組先到達所設定
的目的地即為優勝組。

♠ **教學重點**

　告訴小朋友，在問路時，要先對別人說 Excuse me. 問完之
後要說 Thank you。而別人若對你說 Thank you 時，要回答
You are welcome.

---- 本課重要單字、片語 ----

* gentleman
* department store
* camera
* stranger

* over there
* building
* pleasure trip

習題解答

3-③ EXERCISE (p.20)

A Multiple choice.

1. There are (**some**, any, much) eggs in the basket.
2. We have (few, **little**, many) rain in winter.
3. Mr. Smith is (very, many, **much**) taller than Bill.
4. I have (much, little, **a lot of**) books in my room.
5. There is (a few, **a little**, few) sugar in the cup.

B Make sentences.

1. (usually)

   I usually get up at six o'clock.

2. (often)

   I often go to library on Sunday.

3. (never)

   I am never late for school.

4. (always)

   I always take a walk after dinner.

5. (ever)

   Have you ever been to Hong Kong?

6. (sometimes)

   I sometimes go to the movies with my friends.

UNIT 4

SUSAN'S PEN PAL

♠ 教學目標

教小朋友學會寫一封英文信，並複習「進行式」及代名詞的用法。

♠ 教學方式

(1)老師先在黑板上寫一些現在進行式 $\begin{cases} \text{is} \\ \text{are} \end{cases}$ + Ving 與過去進行式 $\begin{cases} \text{was} \\ \text{were} \end{cases}$ + Ving 的句子，帶小朋友大聲唸。然後給小朋友幾個動詞和時間副詞，指定小朋友起來造現在進行式和過去進行式的句子，老師將小朋友造的句子寫在黑板上，請他們上來改否定句及疑問句。待小朋友都會了之後，再教他們做 p.26 Ⓐ 部分的題目。

(2)用圖表來幫小朋友複習代名詞的主格、所有格、受格、及所有代名詞：

主　　格	所　有　格	受　　格	所　有　代　名　詞
I	my	me	mine
we	our	us	ours
you	your	you	yours
he	his	him	his
she	her	her	hers
it	its	it	×
they	their	them	theirs

(3)在介紹英文信寫法時，老師可先準備一個信封，告訴小朋友如何寫英文信封，和英文地址：

```
（自己的地址）
號、弄、巷、段、街
城市名，Taiwan
R.O.C
                    （收信人的名字）
                    （收信人的地址）
                        街道
                        城市、郵遞區號
                        U.S.A.
```

提醒小朋友，中文地址通常是由大到小，比如說「台北市×路×段×號×樓」，而英文地址却正好相反，由小到大，如 "No.×，Section ×，× Roard／Street，Taipei，Taiwan，R.O.C."，並且要注意寄信人和收信人地址的位置，不要放錯，免得郵差把信寄回你家。

(4)介紹完信封的寫法後，老師可發給每位小朋友一張英文信紙，告訴他們，日期要先寫在右上角，然後左上角再寫 Dear ＋稱謂或名字，之後再寫內容，末了時可加上祝福的話如：Lucky！（祝你好運！）或 Happiness.（祝快樂！）再署上自己的名字。

(5)介紹完信紙寫法的格式之後，老師可敎小朋友把在第一課所學的自我介紹資料拿出來，重新溫習一遍，因爲這是小朋友的第一封英文信，所以要向筆友介紹自己的名字，年齡、嗜好、學校及家庭，自我介紹的資料恰可派上用場。小朋友複習過自我介紹的資料後，老師就可逐句地引導小

朋友寫一封簡短的信，寫完之後，並可讓小朋友輪流上台
來唸自己所寫的信，老師則在旁指導。

♠ 練　習

(1) 老師將每兩個小朋友分為一組，最好是一男一女為一組，
做 p.23 及 p.24 的寫信練習，老師則在旁協助。全班小
朋友都寫完之後，再一組一組輪流上台唸自己寫的信給全
班聽，老師則在旁指導。

(2) 小朋友每2個人一組，每組都準備一樣東西，如鉛筆盒、
卡帶、玩具等，每組輪流上台，向台下小朋友用英文解釋
這件東西是自己的，如 " This book is mine because...."
" This pen is not hers because...." 等。（一定要利
用人稱代名詞。）讓各組小朋友來猜這件東西到底是誰的，
猜對者得一分。最後每組都輪完之後，得分最多的那組獲
勝。

♠ 教學重點

可向小朋友比較過去式和過去進行式的差別。注意無論是現
在或過去進行式，其動詞必須是可持續的才行，如 get on the
bus（上公車）這個動作一下子就作完了，不能持續進行，所
以不可用進行式。

```
───────── 本課重要單字、片語 ─────────

  • member      • wonderful          • test
  • club        • high school        • pen pal
  • understand  • spend ( spent , spent )
  • soon        • be good at
```

4-1 LET'S PRACTICE （p.23）

Look and write.

Dear Lisa,

    My name is Joseph. I live in Taiwan. I am twelve years old. My birthday is on March 10.

    There are five people in my family — my parents, two brothers and me. My father is a teacher, and my mother is a nurse. My hobbies are swimming and singing.

    I am an outgoing boy, and I hope to make good friends with you.

Your friend,

Joseph Lee

2 （p.24）

Dear Joseph,

    Thank you for your letter. I am twelve years old too and my birthday is on December 22.

    I am very shy, because I am the only child in my family. My father is a doctor and my mother is a housewife. My hobby is collecting stamps.

I am glad to be your friend. Please say hello for me to your family.

Your friend,
Lisa Jones

4-3 EXERCISE (p.26)

Fill in the blanks.

A

1. You are __studying__ English now. (**study**)
2. I was __listening__ to the radio then. (**listen**)
3. Your mother is __cleaning__ the room now. (**clean**)
4. Bill and Mike were __running__ in the park then. (**run**)
5. The dog is __sleeping__ under the tree. (**sleep**)
6. They are __watching__ television in the room. (**watch**)
7. Father is __reading__ a newspaper now. (**read**)
8. Mary was __making__ a doll then. (**make**)
9. Jane's brother is __washing__ the car. (**wash**)

B

1. Do you know that man? ⇨ Yes, I know __him__.
2. Did his father meet my brothers yesterday?
   ⇨ No, he didn't meet __them__.
3. Is that Mary's doll? ⇨ Yes, It is __hers__.
4. This car is __yours__. (**you**)
5. The bicycle in front of the store is __mine__. (**I**)
6. Mr. Brown gave __us__ some books. (**Mary and I**)
7. Jane played tennis with __me__ yesterday. (**I**)
8. Whose bicycle is this? ⇨ It is __theirs__. (**they**)

UNIT 5

I AM A DOG

♠ 教學目標

複習形容詞的比較級與最高級的用法，及讓小朋友練習演好一齣英語話劇。

♠ 教學方式

(1) 利用 p.28 的表格，教小朋友將形容詞的原級改為比較級的方法：

① 形容詞＋er／形容詞＋est，如 old, oldest。

② 字尾有 e 則直接加 r 及 st，如 wiser, wisest。

③ 單音節短母音則重複字尾，再加 er 及 est 如 bigger, biggest。

④ 字尾為 y，則去 y 加 ier 及 iest，如 angrier, angriest。

⑤ 三個音節以上，在字前加 more 及 most，如 more beautiful, most beautiful。

⑥ 不規則變化，如 better, best。

(2) 在帶讀課文時，可讓小朋友試著逐句翻譯內文，若遇有小朋友不熟的句型時，則提出來加以複習，以增強小朋友的閱讀實力。

(3) 老師先帶小朋友唸本課的話劇部分，並邊唸邊解釋劇情，劇本講解完後，再將全班小朋友分成兩組，若一組人數不夠 8 人，可由 Daughter 或 Oliver 再飾一角，讓小朋友練

習一堂課，小朋友可以自行設計面具和服裝，於下一次上
課時表演。表演得好的組並可得到老師的獎勵！

♠ 練　習

　　(1) 老師可徵求自願者，或家裡有養狗的小朋友，仿本課課文
　　　　寫一篇 " I am a dog. " 的文章。並於下次上課時上台
　　　　報告。

　　(2) 老師指導小朋友利用身邊的用具一起製作話劇所需的道具：
　　　　① 牆………用厚紙版做成，下面要挖一個洞，讓老鼠 Oli-
　　　　　　　　　　ver 通過，後面用椅子支撐住。演牆的小朋友
　　　　　　　　　　則站在牆後面說話。

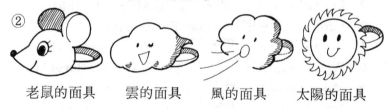

　　老鼠的面具　　雲的面具　　風的面具　　太陽的面具

♠ 教學重點

　　(1) 注意糾正小朋友形容詞比較級及最高級加 er , est 時的發音。

　　(2) 在比較級的句子中，than 後面所接的代名詞必須是主格。
　　　　如 I, he, she 等。向小朋友說明 2 個比較的東西必須相等，
　　　　故 2 個都要用主格來比。

```
───────────── 本課重要單字、片語 ─────────────

• master        • really          • decide

• human         • girlfriend      • husband

• housewife     • the other day   • cover

• in the world  • bride           • look for
```

• shine	• come out	• dear
• blow away	• frightened	• congratulations
• blow down	• frighten	

 智題解答

5-③ EXERCISE （p.34）

Ⓐ Fill in the blanks.

1. Jane is ___taller___ than Mary. (**tall**)
2. My father is as ___old___ as Mr. Smith. (**old**)
3. I got up ___earlier___ than Bill. (**early**)
4. August is the ___hottest___ month in Taiwan. (**hot**)
5. Which is ___larger___ , Taipei or Tainan? (**large**)
6. Mike can run ___fastest___ of all the boys. (**fast**)
7. Your bicycle is ___better___ than mine. (**good**)
8. The pen is ___more___ ___expensive___ than the pencil. (**expensive**)
9. The city is ___noisier___ than the countryside. (**noisy**)
10. Sue is the ___quietest___ girl in our class. (**quiet**)

Ⓑ Read and answer.

Bill is ten years old. Tom is thirteen years old. Mark is fifteen years old. Tom can run faster than Bill. Mark can run fastest of the three.

1. Who is older, Tom or Mark? ___Mark___
2. Who is younger, Mark or Bill? ___Bill___
3. Who is the oldest of the three? ___Mark___
4. Who can run faster, Tom or Bill? ___Tom___
5. Who can run fastest of the three? ___Mark___

UNIT 6

SUSAN WENT TO NEW YORK

♠ 教學目標

複習「附加問句」及「動名詞」的用法，並訓練小朋友用英語簡單地演說「我的志願」。

♠ 教學方式

(1) 老師先在黑板上用現在式寫出動詞，be 動詞及助動詞的例句，幫小朋友複習「附加問句」的改法，再帶小朋友大聲唸，然後指定小朋友上台將這些句子改成過去式及未來式，老師再帶全班將這些句子熟讀。最後將黑板上的句子擦掉，輪流讓學生做口頭附加問句的練習。

(2) 老師可利用第五冊第七課的圖表來複習動名詞的用法。特別是 " Ving＋be 動詞＋形容詞＝It is＋形容詞＋to＋V." 的句型。
　　　　　　　　　　　　　　　　　　　　↓
　　　　　　　　　　　　　　　　　　　不定詞

(3) 老師先帶讀並講解課文會話的部分，然後讓小朋友 3 人一組分組練習（ Officer 和 Steve 由同一人演），二十分鐘後，再分組上台表演，表演特佳的一組，老師可給予獎勵。

(4) 先問小朋友長大之後要做什麼，然後將小朋友想做的事寫在黑板上，再加上本課所列出的各種職業，大聲帶小朋友唸熟。老師在帶讀 p.37 的四則例子之後，可教小朋友仿照這些例子，輪流上台做一分鐘的演講 " I want to be a（an）～ ."

♠ 練 習

(1)將全班分為2組，每次派一位出來猜拳，贏的一方可出題，造一個句子，讓對方造附加問句，若對方答對，則雙方平手，若對方答錯，則扣對方一分。此時，出題者可選擇回答或不回答。若出題者自行回答正確，則可得雙倍的分數，即2分。若出題者自行回答錯誤，則倒扣1分。總積分高者為優勝。

(2)將以前用過的動作圖卡放在紙箱中，讓小朋友一個個上來抽圖卡，依照圖卡的內容造動名詞或不定詞的句型，答對者才可回座，答錯者由老師從旁指導。

> 動名詞＋ be 動詞＋形容詞
> It is＋形容詞＋ to ＋動詞原形。

♠ 教學重點

(1) enjoy、finish 等動詞，後面遇到動詞則要加 ing，如 I enjoy cooking.

(2)
> forgot to ＋ V.（忘記去做某事。）
> forgot ＋ Ving （忘記做過某事。）

> stop to ＋ V. （停下來，去做某事。）
> stop ＋ Ving （停止做某事。）

(3)程度較佳的班級，可為其解釋，附加問句語調的問題：若語尾降低，則表示問的人事實上已經知道答案了，只是形式上再問一次而已。如 "You don't like to go, do you?" 表示對方已經知道你不喜歡去了，只想再證實一下而已。

本課重要單字、片語

- take off
- fasten
- flight

- arrive in
- on time
- passport

6-③ EXERCISE（p.39）

Fill in the blanks.

A

1. Those are your watches, <u>aren't</u> <u>they</u>?
2. Jane is an American girl, <u>isn't</u> <u>she</u>?
3. The man won't come here again, <u>will</u> <u>he</u>?
4. Jim has finished reading the book, <u>hasn't</u> <u>he</u>?
5. Tom's father didn't go to London last year, <u>did</u> <u>he</u>?
6. Helen studies music very hard, <u>doesn't</u> <u>she</u>?
7. You can swim very well, <u>can't</u> <u>you</u>?
8. Mary was busy yesterday, <u>wasn't</u> <u>she</u>?

B

1. I finished <u>washing</u> the dishes. (**wash**)
2. <u>Taking</u> a walk in the morning is good for us. (**take**)
3. Did you enjoy <u>playing</u> cards with your friends? (**play**)
4. <u>Collecting</u> <u>stamps</u> is my hobby. (**collect stamps**)
5. When I came into the room, Tom stopped <u>watching</u> television. (**watch**)

UNIT 7

KEEPING A DIARY

♠ 教學目標

讓小朋友學會如何寫英文日記，及複習被動式：be 動詞＋
p.p 的句型。

♠ 教學方式

(1)老師先利用課本後面 p.70 頁後面的表格，來替小朋友複
習動詞三態，然後在黑板上寫一些主動語態的句子，讓小
朋友自願上來將它改成被動語態，再帶讀這些句子。p.44
的練習，可讓小朋友分組討論，再指定小朋友到黑板上寫
答案。

(2)老師先逐段帶讀課本上的四則日記，並指定小朋友起來解
釋意思，並注意爲小朋友指出重要的時態句型。看完這些
例子後，老師可以問小朋友，如果要他們寫一篇英文日記，
會寫什麼內容，小朋友則舉手輪流發言，老師可以根據小
朋友提出的內容，給予一兩句的提示，然後讓小朋友在課
堂上寫一篇簡短的英文日記，老師則隨時在旁輔導，每位
小朋友都寫完之後，將自己的作品交給老師批改，而老師
在改小朋友的日記時，可叫小朋友分組玩 p.43 的遊戲。

(3)老師改完日記且小朋友玩完遊戲之後，老師將日記發還給
小朋友，讓小朋友訂正完，輪流上台將自己的日記唸給全
班聽，老師並從旁解說批改的地方。

♠練 習

(1) 老師可讓小朋友每個星期交一篇日記上來，由老師批改。每個星期可將優秀的日記，貼在教室佈告欄，或由小朋友上來唸日記給小朋友們聽，慢慢培養小朋友的寫作能力。

(2) 利用第六課練習中的(1)的方式，讓小朋友猜拳，由贏者出題，造一個主動的句子，讓對方改成被動式。

♠教學重點

(1) 修改小朋友的日記時，注意他們標點符號的用法。

```
──────── 本課重要單字、片語 ────────

 • fish                    • exciting

 • field                   • notebook

 • pleasant                • bookstore

 • water                   • hide（hid, hidden）

 • more than               • habit

 • junior high school      • laugh
```

習題解答 **7-1 LET'S PRACTICE**（p.42）

Keep your own diary.

（date）Sunday. July 1.

Today, Mother and I had a very good time. We went to Young & Clean Supermarket this morning. I saw many kinds of food there. After lunch, we

went to see an interesting movie and then went shopping. Mother bought a new dress for me. It looks
very beautiful. I like it very much.

7-2 PLAY A GAME (p.43)

An IQ test.

(1)將每個蘋果切成四塊，共十二塊，每個小朋友就可各得 3
塊蘋果。

(2)

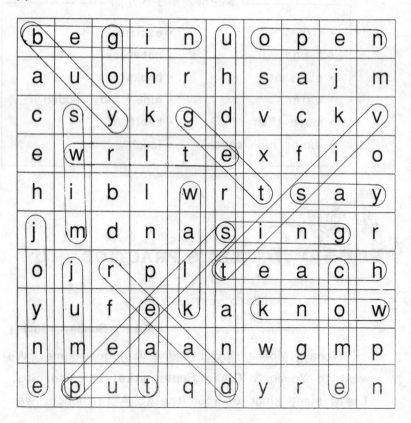

7-③ EXERCISE (p.44)

Change the sentences into passive voice.

1. The man opened the door.
   The door was opened by the man.

2. Tom made these boxes yesterday.
   The boxes were made by Tom yesterday.

3. Father called this dog Lucky.
   This dog was called Lucky by Father.

4. We can see this flower all over the world.
   This flower can be seen all over the world.

5. My uncle gave me a camera.
   I was given a camera by my uncle.

6. They speak English in this country.
   English is spoken in this country.

7. My brother broke the window yesterday.
   The window was broken by my brother yesterday.

8. Tom's uncle caught the lion in Africa.
   The lion was caught by Tom's uncle in Africa.

9. He takes the dog to the park every morning.
   The dog was taken by him to the park every morning.

10. They built a tall building near the river.
    A tall building was built by them near the river.

UNIT 8

TWO SHORT STORIES

♠ 教學目標

本課主要在複習「現在完成式」have（has）＋p.p 的句型。

♠ 教學方式

(1) 利用第二課練習(1)的方式，替小朋友複習動詞三態變化。

(2) 將第 5 冊 p.66 上的句型寫在黑板上，為小朋友複習「現在完成式」。

(3) 老師先帶讀課文中的兩則故事，每句指定一位小朋友起來翻譯。叫小朋友回家將這兩則故事唸熟，於下堂課輪流上台，由老師指定故事，講給全班聽。

♠ 練 習

(1) 讓小朋友玩句子接龍的遊戲，首先由老師指定一個動詞，第一個小朋友造一個現在完成式的句子，第二個小朋友把第一個小朋友的句子重複之後，再用同一個動詞造一個句子，最後面的人要重複前面的人的造句。若中途有人忘記了，則出局，再由老師再指定另一個動詞，重新玩起。

♠ 教學重點

(1) 讓小朋友注意時間副詞 already，just，yet 等在句子中的位置。

————— 本課重要單字、片語 —————

- across   • look at   • ready
- rub   • famous

習題解答   **8-1 LET'S PRACTICE** (p.46)

Look and say.

(1) A : *How long have you studied English?*
   B : *I have studied English for three years.*

(2) A : *How long have you played tennis?*
   B : *I have played tennis for two years.*

(3) A : *How long have you watched TV?*
   B : *I have watched TV for three hours.*

(4) A : *How long have you lived in this city?*
   B : *I have lived in this city for twelve years.*

(5) A : *How long have you waited for the bus?*
   B : *I have waited for the bus for forty-five minutes.*

(6) A : *How long have you collected stamps?*
   B : *I have collected stamps for one month.*

8-③ EXERCISE (p.48)

Fill in the blanks.

1. Bill has just ___opened___ the door. (**open**)

2. Jane has already ___finished___ her homework. (**finish**)

3. They haven't ___eaten___ lunch yet. (**eat**)

4. Has your father ___read___ the book? (**read**)

5. Tom has ___made___ the box. (**make**)

6. Mark hasn't ___done___ his homework yet. (**do**)

7. I ___have___ already ___cleaned___ my room. (**clean**)

8. Tom's mother ___has___ just ___cooked___ breakfast. (**cook**)

9. She has ___told___ us an interesting story. (**tell**)

10. My uncle ___has___ ___studied___ English for two years. (**study**)

11. I have ___known___ Mr. Smith for three years. (**know**)

12. Peter has ___gone___ to New York. (**go**)

13. My sister has never ___driven___ a car before. (**drive**)

14. I've never ___heard___ of it. (**hear**)

UNIT 9

A PRESENT FOR YOU

♠ 教學目標

複習「關係代名詞」who，which，that 的用法。

♠ 教學方式

(1) 老師可先重複第五冊關係代名詞的教法，將兩個相關句子寫在紙片上，重覆的主詞去掉，再用「魔術師」who，which，或 that 來連接。老師可多準備一些寫上句子的紙片，讓每個小朋友輪流上台，對全班表演用關係代名詞將兩個句子連接起來的魔術，並要配合講解。每個小朋友都表演過這個魔術之後，再引導他們做 p.53 的練習，老師每一題可叫一位小朋友起來報他的答案，然後問全班同學的意見，再公布正確答案。

(2) 老師在講解課文之前，可讓小朋友先練習查課文的單字、片語。再由老師舉例解說這些單字、片語，確定他們能活用這些單字、片語之後，再逐句帶小朋友跟讀。並讓小朋友在重要地方畫線。

(3) p.51 的練習，可讓小朋友分組討論，以答題的速度及正確性來決勝負。

♠ 練 習

(1) 將學生分為 2 組，每次輪流派一名出來猜拳，贏的人用中文造一個含有關係代名詞的句子，讓對方用英文譯出來，計分方法如第 6 課練習(1)的規定。最後老師可將雙方都不會的句子提出來講解。

♠ 教學重點

(1) which 代替<u>物</u>（單、複數皆可）

who 代替<u>人</u>（單、複數皆可）

that 代替<u>物</u>或<u>人和物</u>（單、複數皆可）

(2) 可讓小朋友分段背誦課文，幫助記憶句型。儘量用動作提示，協助他們背誦。或以聽寫的方式，寫出課文。

```
――――――― 本課重要單字、片語 ―――――――
 • count（counted, counted）    • dark
 • again                        • silent
 • stand up                     • for a while
 • rich                         • grow
 • take off                     • comb
 • watch chain
```

習題解答

9-1 LET'S PRACTICE （p. 51）

```
 9  Everything is going well.    5  Come here.
 7  I'm full up to here.         6  Oh! I remember.
 3  Good luck; I hope it         8  Me?
    works out.                   1  Oh, I forgot!
 4  I don't know.                2  Wait a second.
```

9-③ EXERCISE (p. 53)

A. Fill in the blanks.

1. The girl __who__ is writing a letter is my sister.
2. Do you know the students __who__ are running in the park?
3. I can't do the homework __which__ was given to us yesterday.
4. The blind man and his dog __that__ are crossing the street live next to us.
5. The cookies __which__ were made by Helen are delicious.

B. Make sentences.

1. Look at the boy. He is swimming in the pool.
   Look at the boy who is swimming in the pool.

2. This is a car. It was made in Taiwan.
   This is a car which was made in Taiwan.

3. Jack is my friend. He lives in Canada.
   Jack who lives in Canada is my friend.

4. I know a boy. He can draw pictures very well.
   I know a boy who can draw pictures very well.

UNIT 10

THE LAST LEAF (I)

♠ 教學目標

讓小朋友自己設計道具及服裝來演一齣話劇,及複習「連綴動詞+形容詞」和「連綴動詞+like+名詞」的句型。

♠ 教學方式

(1) 先利用圖片和例句,來替小朋友複習連綴動詞的用法,老師除了帶讀句子之外,並可拿出準備好的圖片,指定小朋友起來用連綴動詞造句。每個小朋友都造過句子後,老師再利用 p.59 的圖片和問題,指定小朋友起來,用完整的句子回答課本上的句子。

(2) 老師先逐段帶讀,逐段解說課文,儘量多用表情及手勢,讓小朋友感受到故事裏的氣氛。講解完之後,可請小朋友用接力的方式分段將課文唸完。然後再利用 p.56 的問題問小朋友,並可讓小朋友舉手輪流發表對這個故事的感想。

(3) 在講 " Tom Has to Work on Saturday " 時,可先向小朋友介紹「湯姆歷險記」這本書的故事及 Tom 的頑皮性格,先引起小朋友對這個故事的興趣,再配合表演與聲調,帶小朋友讀完並講解完整個劇本(連同 11 課的),然後告訴小朋友表演此劇的要領,Tom 要愈頑皮愈好,小朋友穿的吊帶褲和姑媽的圍裙,都可以增加戲劇的效果。給小朋友多一點時間練習，讓他們培養默契，老師則在旁隨時給予鼓勵及意見。可讓小朋友於下次上課時分組表演。凡是認眞的小朋友，老師都應予以獎勵。

♠ 練 習

(1) 將小朋友分成 2 組，玩「比手劃腳」的遊戲。老師準備數張圖卡，每張寫上一句包含連綴動詞的句子。讓第一組每小朋友輪流上台抽圖卡，依照所抽的句子比手劃腳，讓其它隊友猜所表演的句子。可設定時間，答對較多題的爲優勝隊。

♠ 教學重點

(1) 小朋友在表演話劇時，可爲他們示範每個人物的台詞語調，力求生動活潑，如生氣時，快樂時的語調各有不同。

```
──── 本課重要單字、片語 ────

 • different      • among       • neighbor
 • poor           • get well    • take care of
 • apartment      • will        • fence
 • catch a cold   • vine
```

習題解答

10-1 LET'S PRACTICE（p. 56）

A 1. *They lived in New York.*

2. *She was looking at the leaves on the vine.*

3. *He always said, " Some day I'll paint a great picture."*

4. *Yes, it does.*

5. *They met in New York.*

6. *In November.*

7. *Sue did.*

8. *No, he is an old artist.*

B

Dear Jenny,

    I am sorry to hear that you're sick. Do you know your pictures are very good? I hope you will get better soon, and then draw pictures again.

                        Your friend,
                        Susan.

10-③ EXERCISE (p.59)

1. *She looks pretty.*

2. *It looks like a cat.*

3. *She feels comfortable.*

4. *It sounds exciting.*

5. *It tastes good.*

6. *It smells sweet.*

7. *It sounds boring.*

8. *It tastes like chocolate cake.*

UNIT 11

THE LAST LEAF (II)

♠ 教學目標

教小朋友讀懂一篇故事。並複習「感官動詞＋受詞＋原形動詞」，及「感歎句」的用法。

♠ 教學方式

(1) 老師先寫幾個直述句在黑板上，再告訴小朋友如何將它們改成感歎句，然後將小朋友分成兩組，分給每組 5 句以感歎句拆開來的單字紙片，讓他們在限定時間內把原來的 5 個感歎句拼出來，最先拼完的那組為優勝。遊戲結束之後，老師再引導小朋友獨立將 p.64 A 部分的題目做完。

(2) 課文部分可採與上一課同樣之方式，在此不再贅述。並可叫小朋友回家將課文唸熟，並試著用英文寫出一篇 80 字左右的摘要交上來。

♠ 練 習

(1) 老師先準備好幾張圖卡，上面分別寫上感官動詞及使役動詞如 hear，feel，watch，let，make 等，將小朋友分成 2 組，每組同時派人上來抽卡，並根據上面的動詞來造句，寫在黑板上。2 組不可造重複的句子，計時 20 分鐘，看哪一組造對的句子最多即獲勝。

♠ 教學重點

(1)除了用英文寫日記之外，老師還可讓學生練習寫心得，或故事摘要，訓練寫作能力。

―――― 本課重要單字、片語 ――――

- once
- however
- leaf（leaves）
- soup
- carefully
- probably
- ill
- fall（fell, fallen）
- come along
- stay around
- through

習題解答

11-1 LET'S PRACTICE （p.62）

1. *She said, "That is the last leaf. It will fall today, and I shall die."*

2. *She said, "What a bad girl I was, Sue. I wanted to die. It was wrong. I've learned from that leaf that it's bad to want to die. Now I want to get well and paint pictures again. Give me some soup, please."*

3. *He painted a leaf on the wall after the last leaf fell.*

4. *He went out on the stormy night and caught a bad cold.*

5. *She learned that it's bad to want to die.*

6. *He was ill for only two days.*

7. *He painted it after that last leaf fell.*

8.

> date. Mon. July 2
>
> Today, I read a story "The Last Leaf". It's a touching story. Jenny learned from the leaf that it's wrong and bad to want to die. Everyone should live his life to the fullest. I also respect Mr. Behrman very much. He painted the leaf on a stormy night for Jenny. He is a kind and great artist. I like the story very much.

11-③ EXERCISE （p.64）

A Arrange the sentences.

1. the girl kind is how. ⇨ How kind is the girl !

2. interesting is the story how. ⇨ How interesting is the story !

3. a radio what it small is. ⇨ What a small radio it is !

4. was Helen pretty how. ⇨ How pretty Helen was !

5. what flowers has beautiful she. ⇨ What beautiful flowers she has !

6. bad they boys what are. ⇨ What bad boys they are !

B Make sentences. Use the words given.

① watch　② let
③ make
④ hear　⑤ feel

1. Tom watched the dog eat in the yard.

2. Father doesn't let us play baseball.

3. The program makes Mother feel sad.

4. Peter heard Mary play the piano yesterday.

5. Jack feels the earth shake.

UNIT 12

THE LOVE LETTER

♠ 教學目標

複習 If 的假設句及條件句，及一些購物時的會話。

♠ 教學方式

(1) 老師先在黑板上寫出 If 的條件句和假設句的公式，舉一些
例子來帶讀，並發給每位小朋友一張圖片和兩個相關句子，
要他們依照圖片和句子，造出 If 的條件句或假設句。老師
讓小朋友以舉手的方式輪流出來說他們的答案，造對句子
的小朋友可以回座，而造錯句子的則由老師再加以輔導。
確定每個小朋友都會 If 的句大之後，再帶他們做 p.69 的
練習，每個人的答案可能都不同，老師每題可點幾位小朋
友起來說他們的答案。

(2) 老師指定小朋友起來唸幾句課文，並解釋意思，老師則在
旁糾正發音或更正意思，整課唸完之後，老師再將整個課
文重述一遍，並教小朋友以隔行唸的方式來讀這封信，小
朋友會發現和全文都唸有很不同的意義。

♠ 練 習

(1) 老師和學生一起練習在速食店點餐的會話，由老師當服務
生，請小朋友排隊向服務生點餐。請小朋友事先想好要買
的東西，亦可請老師做一張荣單，讓學生點餐。

(2) 2個小朋友一組，一人當店員，一人當顧客。由老師規定
每一組要購買的東西後，練習二十分鐘。然後輪流上台表
演。練習時，老師可從旁指導。表演最好的一組，老師可
給予獎勵。

―――――――― 本課重要單字、片語 ――――――――

• once	• look forward to	• favor
• dislike	• selfish	• satisfied
• conversation	• foolish	• secret
• boring	• sincerely	• continue

習題解答

12-1 LET'S PRACTICE （p.67）

1 1. A : *May I help you?*
      B : *Yes. What size is this?*

   2. A : *May I help you?*
      B : *Yes. Can I try on this dress?*

   3. A : *May I help you?*
      B : *Yes. Do you have anything larger?*

   4. A : *May I help you?*
      B : *Yes. I'll take it.*

   5. A : *May I help you?*
      B : *Yes. I'll take three of these.*

2 1. A : May I help you?

B : Yes, I want a fishburger and a glass of orange juice.

A : Yes, sir. Is this to go, or will you eat here?

B : I'll eat here, thank you.

2. A : May I help you?

B : Yes, I want an apple pie and a glass of iced tea.

A : Yes, sir. Is this to go, or will you eat here?

B : I'll eat hear, thank you.

3. A : May I help you?

B : Yes, I want a hamburger and an ice cream cone.

A : Yes, sir. Is it to go, or will you eat here?

B : I'll eat here, thank you.

4. A : May I help you?

B : Yes, I want a Coke and French fries.

A : Yes, sir. Is it to go or will you eat here?

B : I'll eat here, thank you.

12-③ EXERCISE (p.69)

1. If I were rich, I would help the poor.

2. If I saw a house on fire, I would call the fire station right away.

3. *If it is sunny tomorrow, I will go on a picnic with my friends.*

4. *If I could drive a car, I would travel all over Taiwan.*

5. *If I were a junior high school student, I would study harder.*

6. *If my classmate is sick, I will go to hospital to see her.*

7. *If I became a monkey, I would stay in the forest.*

8. *If my bicycle were stolen, I would call the police.*

第六册　學習內容一覽表

單元	內　　　容	練　　習	活　　　動	習　　作
複習第五册	1. 我的嗜好 2. 被動式和關係代名詞 3. 一架新的模型飛機 4. 我最好的朋友	Look and read. Make sentences. Look and read. Read and say.		
1	新學年開始	Look and write：讓小朋友練習做簡單的自我介紹，認識班上的新同學。	歌曲：Do your ears hang low？	Write and say.
2	生日禮物	① Look and say：看圖練習用 be going to 來造句。 ② Choose the correct words：選擇正確的過去式動詞。	童詩：Mother Goose.	Fill in the blanks. （複習未來式和過去式）
3	問　路	Find the way：看著地圖幫外國朋友指路。	歌曲：Oh, Susanna！	① Multiple choice. （複習數量形容詞） ② Make sentences. （複習頻率副詞）
4	蘇珊的筆友	Look and write：練習用英文寫一封信給外國的筆友；再以外國友人的身份回信給台灣的筆友。	遊戲：A secret message.	Fill in the blanks. （複習現在進行式和代名詞的所有格、受格等）
5	我是一隻狗	Who is the strongest？ 演一齣英文話劇：「老鼠嫁女兒」，複習比較級和最高級。	遊戲：Biggest, tallest and fastest.	① Fill in the blanks. ② Read and answer. （複習比較級和最高級）
6	蘇珊去耕約	Look and say：請同學上台做小小演說，談談自己的志願。	歌曲：Row, row, row your boat.	Fill in the blanks. （複習附加問句和動名詞）
7	寫日記	Keep your own diary：讓小朋友練習用英文寫日記。	遊戲：An IQ test.	Change sentences. （複習被動式）
8	二個小故事	Look and say：兩人一組，練習看圖一問一答，複習 " How long have you～ " 的句型。	歌曲：Old black Joe	Fill in the blanks. （複習現在完成式）
9	送你的禮物	Look and choose：學習使用英文中的肢體語言，手勢等等。	童詩：Teddy Bear	① Fill in the blanks. ② Make sentences. （複習關係代名詞）
10	最後一片葉子（I）	Answer the questions：閱讀課文後，讓小朋友回答問題訓練理解力。	話劇：Tom has to work on Saturday（I）	Answer the questions. （複習連綴動詞）
11	最後一片葉子（II）	Answer the questions：根據課文回答問題，並將課文要心得記入日記中。	話劇：Tom has to work on Saturday（II）	① Rearrange sentences. （複習感嘆句） ② Make sentences. （複習感官動詞和使役動詞）
12	一封情書	Work in pairs：2人一組，練習用英文在商店中購物及速食店中點餐。	歌曲：Home on the range.	① Answer the questions. ② Fill in the blanks. （複習與現在事實相反的假設語句）
複習第六册	1. 不規則動詞三態變化表 2. 看圖說故事 3. 我的學校生活	Read after your teacher. Tom has to work on Saturday. Write a composition.		

||||||||||||| ● 學習出版公司門市部 ● |||||||||||||||

台北地區：台北市許昌街 10 號 2 樓 TEL：(02)2331-4060・2331-9209
台中地區：台中市綠川東街 32 號 8 樓 23 室
　　　　　TEL：(04)223-2838

||||||||||||||||||||||||||||||||||||||||||||||||

學習兒童美語讀本教師手冊

編　　著／陳怡平
發 行 所／學習出版有限公司　　　　　☎ (02) 2704-5525
郵 撥 帳 號／0512727-2 學習出版社帳戶
登 記 證／局版台業 2179 號
印 刷 所／裕強彩色印刷有限公司
台 北 門 市／台北市許昌街 10 號 2 F　　　☎ (02) 2331-4060・2331-9209
台 中 門 市／台中市綠川東街 32 號 8 F 23 室　　☎ (04) 223-2838
台灣總經銷／學英文化事業公司　　　　☎ (02) 2218-7307
美國總經銷／Evergreen Book Store　　☎ (818) 2813622

售價：新台幣一百八十元正
1998 年 5 月 1 日一版二刷

ISBN 957-519-517-5